My Life's Lantern
Verses and Musings

My Life's Lantern

Verses and Musings

By Margaret Carey

TAMARIND TREE
Toronto

Library and Archives Canada Cataloguing in Publication

Title: My life's lantern : verses and musings / by Margaret Carey.
Names: Carey, Margaret, 1948- author.
Description: Poems and short stories. | Includes index.
Identifiers: Canadiana 20210274441 | ISBN 9781989242087 (softcover)
Classification: LCC PS8605.A7425 M9 2021 | DDC C818/.6—dc23

Cover art: Late Jacek Witecki • ©Bettina Witecki

"In your light I learn how to love.
In your beauty, how to make poems.
You dance inside my chest where no-one sees you,
but sometimes I do, and that sight becomes this art."

- Rumi

Contents

PART II

PART I

WHEN MY LIFE'S LANTERN IS EXTINGUISHED

And when my life's lantern is extinguished, what will there be for me to do?

Perhaps I'll fly away to a magic land where aquamarine waters lap upon the golden sands of Everland.

There I will swim with dolphins and gossip with the mermaids among the coral castles of Atlantis.

Perhaps I'll dance among the treetops with the rogue wind that makes the leaves swoon at his sight and chase the squirrel monkeys as they play.

Or maybe, in the darkest night I'll shimmer to the Aurora disco nights and, while chasing fireflies, watch as my wings become opalescent with a thousand glimmering lights.

I'll scoop up sands of the Sahara in my hand, and let them gently slide between my fingers, just like our life together slipped through pages of the calendar as we were planning our tomorrows.

Maybe I'll lie down with savannah lions in the shade of the acacia tree and watch the cubs wrestling the day away, or run with the wild horses, fingers entwined in the mane of the black stallion, my cheeks red with the wind and my immortal heart beating in rhythm with the hooves.

Perhaps I'll fly with the wild geese and watch the towns below that teem with life, like anthills somewhere on the edge of a forgotten forest.

Or I will float upon the lake, bathing in water and in moon glow, long after the loons have ceased their evening calls to prayer.

I'm certain that I will sleep upon your pillow and leave behind the faintest scent of perfume.

And you, upon the waking hour, will softly call my name believing that I just left your bed.

And when I have cast off my earthly coat, no longer needed in my flight, where shall I go?

Perhaps I'll float in on a moonbeam and gently kiss my babies' cheeks as they, believing this a dream, smile in their sleep letting the calm descend.

Or maybe I will make snow angels in your front yard in the night, or sculpt icicles on eavestroughs to catch the winter prism lights.

One thing I'm certain of; I will not lie beneath the earth, and suffocating wait for visitors to bring me flowers, and light small candles which, flickering for a moment or two, will die upon my chest.

So celebrate my freedom. Please celebrate the lightness of my being, for all too soon it will be time.

And then I'll show you all the places I discovered after I cast off all those heavy robes of life.

A NIGHT TO REMEMBER

Silver ribbons sent down by the moon frolic in the ocean sculpting concentric circles in the inky water, while a choir of cicadas rehearses its midnight recital with rhythmic accuracy.

The tenor bullfrog serenades his lady-love in a rain shower of bold ribbits as a lonely loon sends its mournful anthem to the stars.

You lift my hand slowly and your lips caress each finger as gently as a flutter of a passing thought.

Burying your mouth in the palm of my hand you rest there suffusing my body with tropical warmth.

Your explorations travel upwards toward the crook of my elbow. Softly, you alight there and I sway backwards with the rising heat.

Kissing my shoulder, you map out a path to the side of my neck lingering for a moment at the shell of my ear.

I am now impatient. I watch your eyes as they explore the contours of my face. And then your lips…your lips caress my cheek and find the corner of my mouth.

I want to turn to you, to find the fullness of your mouth, to sink into the warmth, into the nectar, into the softness and the heat.

You hold my face softly in your hands. I yield.. capitulate… fall headlong into oblivion forgetting what or where or why.

The moon plays hide and seek with the passing clouds leaving the sky dark and lost in thought.

You lay me down on the soft blanket at the foot of a house high boulder that decorates the beach.

It is our paravan, our sentinel-the silent witness to our dance.

I spread my wings in readiness for flight and rise to meet you headlong.

A wolf howls in the distance; a chorus answers him in kind.

We rise above the clouds and leave the cares of Mother Earth below soaring on currents of the wind, our faces flushed with the thrill of flight as the beach slowly disappears from sight.

A POEM THAT RHYMES

You make me think of happy things:
of pure white doves and sparkling rings.
      Of fireplaces, of the dew
        that sleeps on grass when day is new.
Of lilac bushes, morning grace,
of careless colts and gowns of lace.
      Of wine that sways in crystal glass,
        of velvet bluebells in the grass.
Of sea that sings a windy song,
of sunlight shining all day long.
      Of kittens with a soft white belly,
        of peanut butter topped with jelly.
Of smells of forest after storm,
of chilly nights with blankets warm.
      Of tiny cottage in the wild,
        of lusty summers, winters mild.
Of teddy bears and diamond streams,
of warm wet sand and future dreams.
      Of peaceful meadows, smell of roast,
        and in the morning: tea, and toast.
Of summer days, of a tanned face,
touch of your hand, a quick embrace.
      Of dusk that steals upon the days,
        of golden wheat in wind that sways.
Of lapping water on the shore,
of hands from work all tired and sore.
      And when I feel the warmth of you
        beside me when the day is new,
And when I taste your mouth so sweet
my happiness and love's complete.

COME WITH ME

Lily pad ice flows down the river
Sluggish and reluctant--grey and greyer still.
   My palm pressed against the window
    melts all the frost around it.
I want to cup your heart inside my hands and warm it with my will.
Icy, dark January slinks into the room.

I feel Death's bony fingers caress my aching throat.
  Life overflows--it melts away all rhyme and reason.
  Like floods of spring, it sweeps away my common sense
  and only candles in the window flicker
  and rise,
  and long to live--proud fire stretching to the sky
  as if tomorrow was another day.
Come with me.

  The sun seems to be setting
  in purple lengthening shadows.
  The long and lonely night will be upon us all too soon.
Come with me.

  There is so little time
  and I have found you just before the sunset.
Come with me.

  The night is almost upon us.

DID YOU KNOW?

Did anyone ever tell you
that your laughter makes all sorrow hide its head in shame
and shadows disappear and light float into rooms like streamers?
    And that your soft voice has the quality of silk
    caressing every contour of my body
    just like a web-light sari?
And do you know that when you touch my hand with yours
a thousand sparks take flight between us
like nighttime fireflies in joyful dance of life?
    And have you heard that at the time your mouth descends on
    mine
    it's springtime once again?
    Inside me bloom eternal flowers; they open up to you with
    dew-drop petals,
    all velvety softness supple under your tongue.
And when you touch my thighs
the sea begins to stir with crests of foam and house-high waves
that fragment on the rocks.
I hear the roar of water in my ears.
It leaves a taste of salt in corners of my mouth.
    With liquid honey of your eyes my only anchor
    I feel I'm swept away into the primitive and encompassing
chant of our two beating hearts.
    My fingers intertwined with yours, our borders are erased.
    Where you once ended, I begin.
At last, when all is still and once again your words caress me
like an arched cat's back against my body,
I rub all my corners against the comfort of your soft laughter in the
night.
    And did you know your laughter…..

FISH ON A HOOK

Suspended animation…. Cinematography frames jammed in a reel – stopped in mid air, in fragments.

You passed me along the way – a blur – Road Runner on his way to a painted tunnel.

I can follow you only in dreams.

Even the sunlight is silent.

****

How did you know that lighted windows are my secret security?

And did you know I've seen Zhivago five times, and still could not lift the veil of sadness that it left behind?

I'm constantly wandering into labyrinths, and when I find a man dressed in the scarlet robes of love even when he harbors an icicle for a heart I'll say: "Ah, but it gives off prism lights that make me want to dance."

****

And now at last, at curtain time, rehearsing all the lines and, most importantly, mouthing the exit, I have it thousand times perfected. This time for the best reasons. This time ruled by the intellect.

And drawing in my breath I turn to you-my speech prepared.

But then my eyes find your mouth and fingers rushing to your cheeks, I find another reason to procrastinate while my heart files the truth into the archives for another day.

Then wrapping myself around you like a vine, drawing the very breath you breathe, I stay within your warmth only to find that morning wants to see me on another train.

FLIGHT

It survives between us – this stubborn ray of belief.
> Despite logic the anger flares up and burns itself out in the
> same instant.
It rises like the morning mist, unfettered and as
certain as the seasons.
> I feel him near me, and I know that my quiet withdrawal will
> not last.
> I wait for his arrival as sure as the day follows night.
I have no reason to believe but without a doubt, I believe,
He will be here.
He is drawn to me; his wings are steadfast in their
course towards my lighthouse heart.
> He will come polarized by the golden speckles in my eyes.
> His course is set.
I feel it on a most primitive level – devoid of any rationale.
> He turns towards me in his sleep reaching
> out for the comforting warmth of my waist.
He turns his head towards the sea which separates us
and twists the gold band around and still around.
A tourniquet, it stops the blood flow to his heart.
A tuning fork, thousands of miles away he quivers
with my vibration.
He has no choice.
He will be here.

I CAN'T BE GRUMPY AT CHRISTMAS

I can't be grumpy at Christmas
Though grumpy I wanna be,
because you can't stay grumpy long around the Christmas tree.
A Christmas tree is cheerful with pretty lights galore
And decorations of all sorts from tree top to the floor.
    I can't be grumpy at Christmas when children laugh and play
      while keeping watch upon the skies, in case they spy a sleigh.
My dear friend Konrad said to me "Our Christmas I deny.
Commercialism's running wild; they're saying 'buy, buy, buy'."
His face was stern and serious-his voice was cold and tart.
But Konrad can't stay grumpy long- he's just a kid at heart.
    I can't stay grumpy at Christmas when twinkling lights abound,
    and Carols ring out everywhere while people mill around.
    I can't be grumpy at Christmas, although sometimes I should.
    I'll send my hubby to the store (he said that go he would)
    The mall is where the presents are and that's where
    him I'll send.
    The Walmart parking lot by now has combat hand to hand.
I can't be grumpy at Christmas when everywhere I see
Santa dressed in a red suit with children on his knee.
I tried to tell dear Santa once, Bentley I wish I had.
He frowned at me and shook his head proclaiming:
"You've been bad".
I don't know how he knows that naughty I have been.
I wonder what are other things the fat man claims he's seen.
    I can't be grumpy at Christmas while food covers the table,
    and family and friends partake of it until they are not able.
    I can't stay grumpy at Christmas: day of a Baby Boy
    It's really all about our faith, our love and our joy.
    That's why I can't be grumpy, perhaps now you can see
    So go in peace and happiness
God Bless your family.

I HAVE LOVED

In the final moments of my life what will I remember as moments of pure love? Here are a few I'll share:

My grandmother's hands — combing my hair, drying my tears, stroking my cheek as sleep comes to claim me once again.

White, white snow decorating tree branches with its soft shimmer.

Hurtling down a hill in a toboggan wind in my face, a tickle of thrill in my chest.

The silver clouds slowly sailing off into the horizon, leaving a clear blue sky.

Water spouting from the mouths of lions in a fountain in a square far, far away.

The tiny tinkling bells on the roofs of the Thai chedi, whispering in the breeze.

White, sugary sands that meet the turquoise seas on uninhabited islands.

The feel of a horse's back beneath me as we gallop down some tropical beach.

Wildflowers, like fragrant surprises, dotting the landscape.

The wriggling and cooing of my babies, newly plucked from my womb, nourished by my body — still a part of me, but so much whole, new beings of their own.

The smell of the forest after the rain.

The call of the loon when the red and gold streamers of the sun announce the end of day.

The touch of a lover's hand.

Soft teddy bears.

The rustle of autumn leaves beneath my feet on an Indian Summer day.

Feel of the ocean around me. Floating, floating, weightless in a giant womb.

Your eyes, dark and sensuous, holding the promise of one more dance in unison as old as the earth itself.

My mother's words when all was lost for me, giving me courage to get up off my knees.

The distant rumble of thunder just seconds before electric zig zags light the sky.

The Northern Lights in colourful display delighting the Rocky Mountain wilderness as we lie together and alone on the soft grass beyond the campsite.

My dog's calm breathing as she lies curled up against my belly.

The soft growl of the Harley as I ride alone with summer wind as my sole companion.

The night lifting its velvet curtain off the Sahara as the sun casts shadows on the sandy dunes around us.

Music that lifts and calms and fortifies. Above all music, my faithful and constant friend.

Laughter. Laughter until the tears roll down our cheeks.
The smells of Christmas: of fir, of cinnamon and cloves, and freshly
baked cookies.

The crackle of wood on the fire; its ribbons of smoke rising to the
endless skies.

Lying wrapped in your arms, entwined, and spent and fragrant.

And most of all, the eternal gift of blank pages of new days, waiting
to be filled with stories of my life.

I LOVE YOU

(With Apologies To Elizabeth Barrett Browning.)

I love you with a calm beating of my heart, yet with the
 knowledge that our paths might never cross again.

> I love you on weekdays and on Sundays when lazy dawn
> stretches in the hallway
> and birds chatter incessantly in the lilac bushes.

I love you in the park under the chestnut tree
and on the busy street amid the dancing, whirling crowd.

> I love you in the evening bathed in the glow of candles
> when sun's red and golden rays caress the mother earth

I love you when I walk my dog and when my footprints
mark the freshly fallen snow.
When I'm buying bread and when I dial a number on the telephone.

> I love you when other arms hold me while I dance
> and when alone I kneel in prayer.

I love you in the middle of the day when daily chores
seem to fill my mind,
and in the gray hours of the morning when sleep, bored
by its night-watch, suddenly leaves my bed and
only the clock ticks away its murmurings.

> I love you on the two-lane highway and on the grassy knoll,
> in sea salt spray of a blue ocean, and in the company
> of desert Bedouins.

I love you on a horse when the wind plays with
my hair and when the rain pelts against the windowpane.

I love you while I kiss the silken heads of my children and
when the snowflakes come to rest upon my eyelashes
on a brilliant and silver day.

I love you in my loneliness and when deep in thought I plan my day.
I love you when drowsy from a dreamless sleep I sip
a cup of coffee and after work, when peeling the
potatoes, I drift back to the halcyon days of our youth.

I love you in a sweater and in flannel pajamas; in front of the
television and in the cinema; in the airplane and on a bicycle.

I love you since the early innocent years melded
our lives together,
and I will love you until the end of my journey on this planet
when with my last breath I will recall the mountains
and the forests which once, in a real-life fairy tale,
united our footprints in that faraway land of our childhood.

I REMEMBER YOUR FACE

I remember your face.
> All the smooth valleys, all the emery board rough plains traced with
> my fingers in the sunsets and sunrises of our days together.

I can retrace its paths in my mind's eye without a pause or hesitation.
> I remember your eyes, dark and brooding as the skies
> of rainy November, the tiny lines multiplying in the
> corners when your laughter filled our house.

I saw myself reflected in your eyes; all my imperfections made perfect by their prism. Their darkness like buckwheat honey mellow and liquid was my asylum; there I could bathe naked in the star splashed night with the Casseopia constellation as my only witness.
> I remember your hands, smooth like petals of Salpiglossis;
> strong like the columns of Apollo.
> Your hands held my face with the gentleness of an artist
> painting a fresco on an eggshell.

I remember your mouth, soft as a song of a meadow lark. Your mouth whispering my name as the moon slumbered on our sofa.
Your mouth explored the secret, holy places of my body with reverence and delight.
> I remember your hair, dark and thick and coarse as a Blue Roan's
> mane, my fingers entwined in it as I rode against the wind on some
> forgotten beach.

I remember your chest, the place to rest my head and fall asleep to the rhythmic beating of your valiant heart while I breathed in the familiar scent of leather and cologne.
> I remember your back, strong as a gladiator's, as you
> walked into the night turning around to see me once again.

I remember that night like it was yesterday.
> The night wept in the treetops as it bore witness to our last goodbye.

I WAIT

In futile, furtive moments
glancing at pictures glancing back,
I wait for footsteps in the hall.

    Birds perching on the railing
    tilt their heads, approach my statue stillness.

Some overlapping circles of memories
disturb my eyelids
and reaching out I start to realize
I'm clutching heartbeats.

    Remembering your scent
    I flush and run towards another misused hour
    knowing that it will fuse with others into a misused day.

So paralyzed by your absence,
I analyze the dripping of the tap
unable even to lift my head towards a prayer.

    My life, my lover, turn back and kiss
    the lethargy of silence that numbs my limbs.

And let me wrap my limbs around your tree trunk
So I can live and feel and hurt again.

I WISH FOR YOU

I wish for you tranquility;
The sounds of piano nocturne
Coming through the open windows of an ivy covered cottage.
    I wish for you peace of mind;
    the golden glow of sunset turning the pond to embers,
    concentric circles from pebbles thrown into its calm
    entwined like our fingers in the night.
I wish for you the quiet;
sitting under the broad oak's shade,
pasture sounds coming through a curtain of sleepiness,
cow bells in the distance,
a jack rabbit with ears straight up, paws tucked in
listening to the meadow before he disappears.
    I wish for you the calmness;
    stars splashed across the canopy as if by some divine mistake.
    A fire softly glowing,
    wine swaying in crystal glasses,
    our bodies warm from the day's sun
    lulled by the forest sounds.
I wish for you
long walks in the woods, barefoot splashes in the stream,
the soft licks of a dog in the morning,
and your children's arms around your neck.
    I wish for you laughter out loud,
    the sacred ability to cry mingling your tears with another's,
    and the undying bond of friendship.
But most of all
I wish you love
that you can return day after glowing day
until your back is bent with many years.
    I wish for you tranquility
    of growing older, wiser, stronger
    through all the peaceful and content
    days of your life.

JOURNEY'S END

It's been a long and tiring journey through the seasons,
with pallid dawns and red rimmed dusks, and velvet nights
that found me howling in despair with arms uplifted
towards the unforgiving face of Ancient Moon.

    Life flowed sometimes like rhythm of the rails,
    sometimes like plasma--turning days into years
    without regret, rehearsals, or an intermission.

I practiced all the rituals of love, danced in its hallways
and traced all of its steps in snow and in the sand.
I wounded hearts with unrelenting silence and
fled without "good-byes".

    Then suddenly and without a fanfare, I saw you in the doorway.
    Without time to even straighten out my crinolines I stood
    transfixed.
    The sun was at your back, your face in shadows.

And all I could do was shiver at the lightest brief caress
of your soft voice against my skin.

    Today, the circle of your arms is my real hideaway.
    Today, I place in your hands my glittering and fragile heart
    trusting that you won't let it slip and shatter
    into a thousand pieces of the puzzle
    I find my life to be.

KISSES, GIVEN AND RECEIVED

Soft as wings of a butterfly landing on your bare shoulders, warm, sensual, and sweet kisses surprise you as you wake.

Tiny Ivory Snow scented feet of a new, precious life kick joyfully as you plant small kisses them. In the corner of the room beggar-time watches amused.

Your hand caressing the soft fur is surprised in the waning light of day by a sandpaper scrape. Wanting to withdraw it you stay anyways enduring the emery board love of sweet kitty kisses.

Rodeo Drive on a hot summer day with its colours and sounds bakes in the sun. Women bejewelled, pulled, and painted, descend from their Ferraris and Bentleys to greet each other with perfect California air kisses. "Mwah, mwah" hangs in the air. Not even the lightest buss allowed for fear of smudging such perfection on the California stage.

Ooof, the dreaded moment arrives in the form of Aunt Gretchen. As she materializes in the hallway of your house, her formidable rolls of fat billow like sails in the sunset and a cloud of lavender assaults your delicate nasal mucosal membranes. She sails towards you starched and delicately moustachioed, a defect you discover as she brings her cheek down to receive your humble and imperative kiss.

Perfunctory is what springs to mind as two who would rather be anywhere except together, prepare to leave the house on the way to their individual activities. Lips tightly closed, their goodbye kiss is brief, pained, and full of secret dread one feels awaiting the drill of a dental root canal.

The old-fashioned hand-written letter, its paper subtly scented with perfume, having gone the way of the Dodo bird can now be sent through a computer. Its last line marked with many X's delivers virtual yet silent and sterile kisses.

The doors close with a dreaded finality. He waits on the platform in a manly wide legged stance, fighting the urge to give in to the inevitable show of sorrow. She leans out of the window of the train as it slowly pulls away and touches her fingers to her lips blowing the last kiss towards the quickly disappearing figure of the man she loves.

They come in droves. The privileged ones approach the throne, kneel down with eyes appropriately downcast and, as a grizzled hand extends towards them, they reverently and gratefully kiss the large imposing ring.

The night is tropical and steamy. The ocean's eternal song hypnotic in its primitive simplicity washes over them. Mouths seek each other impatiently and finding their mark, sink deeper and deeper into forgetfulness as primitive and overwhelming as a siren song. Whispers and sighs accompany the deep, slow, soft, and urgent kisses; kisses that open the locked doors to a momentary paradise.

Kisses given and received in love, in sorrow, in obligation, in joy, in laughter, in passion.
Kisses-our comfort and companion; our human fulfillment of the need to connect.

MELANCHOLY

In the waning light of an autumn day, Melancholy wafts into the room
on the wings of a forgotten song.
It wraps its silvery shawl around my shoulders and whispers just one word in my ear:
Your Name.
The name I called out in the night while your soft kisses erased it from my lips as calendar pages fluttered and fell to the floor.

Melancholy, disguised as a gray dove which perches somberly on tombstones in the rain, sits in the corner painting a picture of that familiar beach.

The sea is gentle and forgiving. Turquoise and transparent it washes away our sins without requesting penance.

I fold into your waiting arms: my fortress and my hideaway.
I am that last piece of the puzzle which fits so easily into your heart.

Melancholy, dressed in a cape of smoky sadness, hums a wistful tune as dusk descends upon the room.

I hear your heartbeat, my ear pressed against your chest, as you stroke my hair and softly call my name.

A dog barks in the distance; a car horn blares its disapproval.

Melancholy rises slowly. Spreading her silver wings she dissipates in the waning light while shadows dance on walls of my solitary cell.

I am alone again.

I'm told that you will bring me home after the last grain of sand falls in the hourglass.

And with that quiet thought, I walk away content.

MIST

The days allotted to us float by and burst like bubbles leaving behind a shadowy imprint of their fragile beauty.

Memories float by in the garden forming familiar shapes, like a brass rubbing coaxed into life by an artist's hand.

I move towards you- a somnambulist with starlight splashed across my shoulders, half-hypnotized but all aware of every sound you make.

I am a tuning fork; too many miles away I quiver with your vibration.

Sitting under a canopy of trees in the glow of silver moonlight I'm slowly disappearing like the ebbing tide.

Soon I'm as transparent as a drop of morning dew, light as a puff of smoke and voiceless like a mountain.

The moon, curious and amused by my changing form kisses my hair and sends down a cape of silver moonbeams.

I wrap it tightly around my shoulders.

The silvery ribbons come alive with memories which stroke my face and hands as gently as the brush of an owl's wing in its silent flight.

I'm weightless now, willingly soaring above the cares and sorrows of the past, tumbling headlong into a dreamless, gray, and final slumber.

NIGHT OF THE NEEDLEPOINT

Rain splashes against the window with droning, rhythmical persistence.
Some long-forgotten nocturne plays in my mind's eye, stealthily
travelling into my fingertips.

Like strings on a marionette, memories tug at my limbs-turning me
round and around as I begin to dance, no will left of my own.
Your laughter splinters like broken glass- prisms of light making me
catch my breath as with a sharp pain.

The needle in my fingers travelling through the canvas now has a life
of its own.
My fingers hypnotized by the void long to touch your face.

They move as in a trance guiding the woolen threads, unwilling or
afraid to break the pattern now.
Your mouth descends softly on mine; softly, then with more
persistence. And slowly catching fire I flare and arch towards you.

Running to meet you headlong I'm swept up into your waiting arms.
A dog howls in the night.

I spin back riveted to my silence.
The tap drips rhythmically.

The fridge hums.
Your hands on my thighs are lifting me to your mouth.

I drown inside you, flying as you take me higher than I have ever
imagined I could fly.
I want to bury my face in the small of your back.

I want to sleep inside your scent moulded to you, our breathing peaceful
and content.
I will wait out the night.

OCTOBER NIGHT

I lie awake and wide-eyed, beyond the point of being tired, longing to bathe in unmindful waters of the river Lethe.

    A stranger to my fears, you lie consumed by a dreamless sleep.
    Your stomach like a swayback mare rising against the hollow
    of my back.

The night is pale-it dresses up like dawn between the curtains.
A starless, windless, chilling autumn night devoid of lapping sounds of water: my secret womb security.

    The fire crackles.
    It explodes.
    A log falls forward with a jangle burning me inside.
    It spreads like plasma all around devouring wood and paper.

I'm empty of all joyous thought and hypnotized, watch the flame suffocating with a certain and malicious frown.
It's trapped under an ember and struggling free, consumes itself.
Pale smoke curls upwards like party-ribbons announcing its death.

    Another step towards Nirvana.

The night, bright eyed, stares shamelessly into the window.
It strokes my hair with icy fingers.

    The embers glow like rotor-fanned red light bulbs.

Trees, mere skeletons, thin and fragile, cringe from the rising wind.
The cold air, swirling around my ankles like a creek, creeps through the cracks in woodwork and settles confidently for the night.

    Small sounds beyond the room: a grunt, a snore, a creak seem
    unaware of devil wind making the river dance.

The embers glow vaguely like discontent within their prison, conquered and tamed by our will.
I will not desecrate them by poking at their guts.

    Returning to your bed with small sighs, I watch you rise and
    fall. A mollusk-a slave to your addictions.

I close my eyes twice frightened by the night.

ON THE RUNWAY

And so, we laugh, and cry, and love, and take care of things, and wonder what the hell it's all about.

And we find that to love feels better than to hate, and to feel peaceful feels better than to feel angry, and to lovingly help another being human or animal, feels a whole lot better than to hurt or destroy one. And that through adversity we learn to be patient and strong, and slowly the whole thing begins to come together.

And then it is no longer about gathering things, but about extending love to those who need it the most.

And as we learn, and as we grow, the faces in the mirror become softer, the tiny, darling wrinkles become not so darling, the once luminous and taut skin begins to lose its elasticity, and the hair turns whiter. But somehow, it's O.K., because we know that it all has not been wasted. That, in spite all those mistakes made, and all the wrong turns taken we're growing, we're learning, we're softening. And even though time passes with lightning speed, we're beginning to feel on our shoulders the sprouting of wings.

•••••••••

Love does not demand love in return; it exists merely for the purpose of giving. It must not be dressed up, put on display, chained down or given conditionally. Some of us love quietly without a fanfare or even acknowledgement.

Some of us love creatures most in need of loving: the abandoned, the sick, the deformed, the unwanted and unloved. To gather those creatures to your heart is the highest and purest form of love. To love the old, the unlovable, the ugly, those who strayed from the path, to love for giving of love alone, that is the purest form of love.

To love the trees and the grasses and the earth for its unending and boundless generosity, to love all creatures from the busy ant to the graceful cheetah, from the frightening octopus to the graceful dolphin, that is the purest form of love.

Love for love's sake that is what it's all about.

OUT OF THE SHADOWS

It's been a long and steady journey from innocence
through prism of experience and down the corridors of life.
It taught me to allow the unchangeable to remain unchanged
and not reach too often to rattle the chains that bound me.
>It's been a journey through the seasons:
>from pallid dawn to red rimmed dusk.
>And sometimes I allowed myself the luxury of howling in
>despair (or joy) into the unforgiving face of ancient moon.
Life flowed some days like rhythm of the rails,
some days like plasma. Spreading without regret.
And days turned into years without an intermission.
>I practiced all the rituals of love,
>danced in its hallways and traced all of its steps
>in snow and in the sand; in light and shadow.
>Scraped hearts with unrelenting silence,
>and shattered dreams with all my swift departures.
I laughed out loud and cried too often at all these dress rehearsals.
>And then, without a fanfare or even time to straighten out my
>crinolines
>I saw you in the doorway.
>The sun was at your back-your face in shadows,
>and all I could do was shiver at the lightest brief caress
>of your soft voice against my skin.
>And like a child again so many merry-go-rounds ago,
>I wanted to sit with you at every sunset,
>describing with great pride and joy
>everything I did that day.
The circle of your arms is my real hideaway
as in your gentle hands I place my glittering, immortal heart,
throwing all caution to the wind.
Prepared perhaps for the last fall into despair,
but never giving up eternal hope that you will keep it as your treasure
and never let it slip and shatter into a thousand pieces of the puzzle
I find my life to be.

PASSION REMEMBERED

The evening paints the city with turquoise shadows.
The moon, full and sensuous plays with the clouds.

Like splintered glass, moments glitter in my mind.

I try to trace your face with fingers of my mind's eye, memory my only tutor.

Watching the clock I listen to the endless dripping of the tap and slowly feel myself fold up into my inner being, back to the embryonic form, back to the weightless womb.

Floating in darkness are images of your hands.
I touch them with my fingertips and trace their lines with smoothness of my tongue.

The night intrudes again, moon whispering like forest winds.

My hair, splashed on a pillow as with a painter's careless brush, dark as longing itself, gets crushed like petals in your hand.

Your mouth, tracing small pathways down my belly sends tiny shivers up my spine.

Feeling your weight, I glide with smoothness of one autumn leaf into the dark and damp reality,
and eyes riveted to the clock I watch the second hand
moving towards the minutes,
moving towards the hours,
moving towards the days
when I can warm my soul within the circle of your arms.

A POEM FOR RYAN

Ryan is a super boy:
Grandma's special pride and joy.

    He likes going to the park
    But runs home when it gets dark.

Every day he goes to school
Where he learns about the rules:

    When to play and when to learn
    When to share or take a turn.

Ryan loves to play with trains
When it's sunny or it rains.

    Favourite train of his is blue
    And the name is Thomas –true!

Thomas wheels around the track,
Then our Ryan has a snack.

    Toast and cheese and carrots crunch
    Ryan loves these foods to munch.

Every poem has an end,
So goodbye for now, my friend.

SPRINGTIME

When your mouth finds the hollow of my neck,
it's like the peace of autumn sunset
that paints the leaves which twirl in silence to the ground.
> And when your fingers lightly stroke my back,
> it's like a summer evening's storm:
> rain falling in torrents,
> birds hiding in the trees- unfinished songs still in their throats.
> Only the distant, rumbling thunder disturbs the easy
> fragrant silence.
And when you gently lay me down,
your eyes liquid and mellow
remind me of the sea's foamy crests that ebb and flow like heartbeats.
The fragrance rises musky and electrically sensual.
> And when our bodies blend together-
> hands and mouths seeking each other,
> we fall from grace into impatience.
> Then arching like a cat I stretch
> to meet you headlong.
It's springtime once again.
> The blooms, tightly closed and green, in time-lapse photography
> relax
> and open.
> and dripping dew
> bask in the sun.
Birds, in frenzied symphonies
announce their joy to the whole forest.
There are scents of pine and earth,
ferns swaying in the breeze,
and fox cubs out for their first look
at the green, waking, shimmering world.
> Your mouth on mine…..
It's springtime once again-time of beginnings,
time of the dance of life and, once again,
time of eternal hope.

THAILAND

Everywhere I go here, I feel the comforting presence of someone or something very protective.

A great peace descends upon me as heavy as the scent of jasmine around my neck.

Peace – from the tinkling of the brass bells on the roof of the chedi to the stillness in the "second path" in the monks' quarters.

From the dark, star-lit nights in the north with their mist that rises off the rice paddies in the morning, to the kaleidoscope of the coral reefs in the Andaman sea in the south.

From the early morning crow of the roosters to the steady roll of the elephant's shoulder blades under your feet beneath the canopy of the singing jungle.

From the mournful wind instruments old as Siam itself to the little bending wrists of the Thai dancers.

From the serene face of the Buddha to the flower laden frangipani trees among the ruins of the Burmese invasion's aftermath.

From the upturned face of a Thai baby on my lap to the song of the giant night insects.

The peace of the temple, the peace of the mountains, the peace of the ocean.

I am lulled by it.

I unfold in its presence and warm my aching, broken wings within its glow.

THE ARTIST'S PRAYER

Oh, Great Spirit of the Universe,
We have been brought together
By the Hand of Divine Coincidence
That hears our prayers of longing
And gently guides us into the path of light.

Help us open up to Your Will
As flower buds of May open their petals to the sun.

We extend our Artists' hands, hearts and minds to You
So You may fill them with enlightenment
As it begins to cascade in us, and through us
Onto the parched and cracked ground
Of Blessed Mother Earth.

And in becoming vessels for Your Will
May we expand in knowledge and in love,
Supporting each other, and lovingly keeping
Our Lighthouse Beacon Hearts
Shining streamers of knowledge
to those still lost at sea.

THE DREAM

I dreamt about you last night: a broad chested stranger on the periphery of the circle of laughter, amused and accepting, mellow and crackling with latent sparks of spent adventures.

You were there like my safety net for I could look at the sea of faces and be calmed by your posture.

> Later, running into your arms, enveloped like Linus by his blanket or a porpoise on a sand bar by life giving sea, I folded into you like a tired child, my head upon your chest, your lips upon my forehead and all was well again within the world.

Inside the room, our kisses like dry tinder one breath away from catching fire, carried the promise of oblivion.

> But the glass door reminded us that we must wait to carry our passion for each other until the dark of night. Only then would you sweep me up upon the black-eyed stallion I gave you as a wedding gift.

With my head crowned by wildflowers which you hand-picked on that very day, my cheeks flushed with promises of sunset, I melded into you as we galloped along the border of the sea until the pink and orange streamers announced the break of day.

> Upon my waking the dream began to dissipate, diffuse and dim like theatre lights, like morning fog. Its ends began to fray.

Your face faded into the light and all along my hands trembled with sorrow at the loss.

> Yet in my heart remained a spark, a promissory gift left by your shadow much like a laurel wreath of hope which I picked up ever so gently and placed upon my temples for the day.

THE EXIT

And now at last, at curtain time,
rehearsing all the lines and
most importantly, whispering the exit,
I have it thousand times perfected.

This time, for the best reasons;
This time ruled by the intellect.

And taking in a sigh I turn to you-
My speech prepared.

Then my eyes find your mouth.
My fingers rush to your cheeks- find reasons to procrastinate.
Enveloped in your warmth
my heart won't make room for the truth, but
understanding
files it into the archives for another day, or rather
(whispering lies)
for just another hour.

And wrapping myself around you like a vine,
drawing the very breath you breathe,
I stay within your warmth only to find
that morning wants to see me
on another train.

THE LEASH

Inevitably, irrevocably, arrived The Time of Goodbye.
I heard its lowly rumbling approach like so many tanks rolling
outside my window in the innocence of childhood.
I heard the distant, thundering approach.
I watched it draw near, paralyzed by its self-assured stride.
Months of silence.
Capitulation.
Head hung in helpless abandonment.

I gather the torn rags of what once were my royal robes.
I gather them up, and with that armful head for the door.
No hand on my shoulder stops me.
No whispers, shouts of protest reach my ears.

I walk away from the chains that bound my wrists and ankles,
the collar still around my neck, leash dragging on the floor.
I turn the rusty doorknob silently.
I'm free.

•••••••••••••

The number on "call display" did not look familiar.

His voice…. the velvet of his voice swept over me like a quiet storm.

He yanked my leash – picked it up as it dragged behind me, and
gently stopped me in my tracks.

I strained to move forward.
It took my breath away.

I stopped and stood very still, hesitant to look behind me.

THE MERMAID

Halogen moon drawing me to its heart
illuminates the aquamarine depths of soft and beckoning waters:
Mystic Mermaid Asylum...

> My throat glistens with dew of summer's heat,
> and diamond sweat-drops sigh between my breasts.

Visions of lips and thighs that move in silence, riding me like the endless
summer wind – bridled and free, shimmer behind my lids.

> The castles in the sea beckon me into their crystal hallways
> and as I lean into their mirrors, the moon does stroke my back.

The icy glare of Winter Solstice glazes the pavement of some familiar
highway...

> But here, in silence, the moon bathes sensuous and cool.

I dare dream of neon nights before the scales did bind my thighs when,
having risen to your lips, I entered knowingly and blindly into the
rickety and slippery hell of all your indecisions.

THE PITFALLS OF BEING A MISTRESS

You have come into my life most certainly creating a seiche in the waterbed of my reviviscent heart.

My cobwebbed emotions undulate like a nun's wimple causing a tempest in the pell-mell of my viscera.

Visions of your round psychrophilic spouse dance in my head like sugar plums, spurring me towards hoydenish and obstreperous behaviour.

I teeter now between a rhadamanthine sequestration and projected thoughts of uxoricide attained with aid of muscarine, and thus enter gladly into the mystic, Chthonian Underworld while "facilis descensus Averno" sonorously rings in my head.

••••••••••••••••

Alas, civility subjugates desire and I retreat into the queue that leads to resolution.

With wind no longer in my sails, I remain steadfastly yours.
The Capricious Regulus of Your Symbiotic Fifth Sign,

Regulus Itself.

THE SEA BETWEEN US

It survives and thrives– this stubborn ray of belief,
despite logic and despite the anger that flares up and burns itself out in
the same instant.

It rises like the morning mist, unfettered and as certain as the seasons.
I feel him near me, and I know that my quiet withdrawal will not last.
   I wait for his arrival as sure as the day follows night.

Without a doubt I believe:
He will be here.
He is drawn to me. His wings are steadfast in their course towards my
lighthouse heart.
He will come, polarized by the golden speckles in my eyes.
His course is set.

I feel it on a most primitive level – devoid of any rationale.
Turning towards me in his sleep he reaches out for the comforting
warmth of my waist.
He turns his head towards the sea which separates us, twisting the gold
band around and still around.

A tourniquet, it stops the blood flow to his heart.

A tuning fork, thousands of miles away he quivers with my vibration.
He has no choice. He will be here.

TWO STRANGERS

I long only for darkness: the hour of witches, goblins, fear,
to flow against my eyes and block the sounds and sights and feelings
while running its silent, tired fingers
over my face and hair, just like a mother of a grieving child.
  I think that the calm evening erases all your words like footprints
  along forgotten beaches with nothing more but time.
Unlocking the Pandora's Box
I never felt so lonely as when I heard your words
a thousand miles away.
A million smiles away, you fled my consciousness
and finally led me to believe
that this time, after all the time,
at last,
we have become two strangers.
  I've never seen your eyes light up with such a multitude of neons.
  All of a sudden you were free, and I was silent once again
  repeating in my throat:
  "Lord, let me mend my broken wings"
  like some outdated formula for happiness.
The darkness- my enemy, my lover, envelopes me slowly in its arms
and I, like tiger alley cat
rub all my corners on its warmth
and calm the tears behind my eyes
without your kisses or your light.
  We stand apart
  and look each other up and down like new encounters-
  slightly hostile, slightly frightened,
  but most of all, indifferent.
I've had no better friend tonight.
  The water splinters on the rocks in bitterness and rage.
  The old whore-evening kisses my forehead
  and slips a thought into my hand.
I walk away content.

UN...

More silently than age
Unseen, unheard, unnoticed and uninvited
it steals upon your heart and when you're unaware
it blinds your soul with unexpected light.

> Unfettered it shows its face in shadows and in clouds.
> You feel its undeniable presence like a crown of thorny roses –
> fragrantly soft and painful all at once.

Unhampered it brings ecstasy and unimaginable joy,
carrying with it a glow that warms your weary days.

> Unequaled and unfathomable since life on earth began,
> it fills your heart with faith in all tomorrows.

Unconcerned it sees you whistling around corners at cats and pigeons,
uncaring that clouds have gathered heralding the approaching rain.

> Unequivocal it endows you with all the mysteries of the world:
> Pythagoras is an amateur; you–an unerring genius.

Unexpurgated it plants within you a promise of infinity.
Thus, unperturbed you give it reins and soon you fall into the abyss of
its ruthless lies.

> Unmeaning it leaves the life that knows or feels or sees it not.
> Until one day, undaunted and unoffending (or so it seems)
> it tires of that game with you
> And….
> Unpardonable it slips away while you lie sleeping.

In darkness of the night, it steals away
unrivaled, unruffled, unswerving and untraceable,
leaving you nursing unleashed and unbearable grief
day after unrequited day.

> Until, with turning of the pages of your calendar,
> Unparalleled, unsparing, untiring and unrelenting,
> It finds a quiet space as an unyielding sliver in your heart.

VALENTINE'S DAY
(As Seen By A Disgruntled Lover)

February – the very skeleton of the year.

Stripped of greenery, surrounded by a tomb of clouds, February chills us to the core.

To pump life into it, someone invented a red heart holiday.

A forced lovefest delighting peddlers of anything deemed as romantic, it strong-arms us into the corner painted over with two dimensional pink hearts.

For twenty-four hours of Valentine Love lovers love each other more, spouses frantically search for their lost passion, and children in grade school exchange cards with those whom they like, mortally wounding those they don't by their cruel omission.

On that day lonely people hide away and, in the silence broken only by their tears, try to remember when love was theirs; when every day was lived in colour and sights, smells and sounds delighted all the senses.

Then they could soar above the clouds on magic carpets woven from their lovers' words and touch the face of The Immortal in the kaleidoscope of rapture.

Then Valentine's night was filled with chocolate truffle sighs and champagne bubble laughter, and the rose petal touch of skin on skin would mix with cinnamon sting of candy hearts upon the tongue.

Valentine's Day-a panacea for the gray, sad month of February.

Maybe in March love will come, clad in humble clothing and without a fanfare but with a true, valiant heart on its sleeve.

WE'RE BACK TO THAT AGAIN

We're back to that again.

I'm murmuring that once more your words have maimed me
with their practiced bow.

Then with a sorrow small as a wounded bird's whose leg was snapped
in two by wicked hands,
I'll whisper lamely
that your lies, lies, lies have grieved me.

And I will cry invisible streams of sorrow for all I knew when the tide
was low,
recalling mirrors of my soul which memorized the pages of my life.

I'll stand amazed, perplexed at visions forming like wicked vapour
from the burning mouth of Etna
exhaled by my mind's eye

And then I will transform: a chameleon born on the Night of Eden,
much like a dream you once dreamed centuries ago
on that first eve of your renewal.

And you will thirst to grasp my vision
like sobbing Aenas reaching out for his Creusa among the flames.

But I will fade with crowing of the cock.

Like the dew, like a ring of smoke I will die.

And soft in your eyes a suffering will shine,

but you won't bleed.

The blood is always mine.

WHY?

And so again, the time has come
when I would gladly howl with pain
and pull my hair and rock like peasant women do.
  But only a low and piteous yelp escapes my lips
  as simple motions rule my body-repetitive and numbing.
Now all my prayers have changed their course
simply invoking endurance.
  I am weakening, trembling, and faltering.
I should not have knelt so long at the overgrown grave of my dreams,
for now the pain throbs in my temple.
  Burning within the shade, I long to look into the sun to
  be struck blind for having seen too much
  while questions whirl inside my head.
What winding course has been assigned to me?
  Why laurel thorns? Why empty boxes?
Why bitter fruits? A tattered bridal veil?
  Why babies lost to me? Was it too early or too late?
Why a house of cards in the eye of a hurricane?
  Why boats made out of toothpicks in sea of house high waves?

    •••••••••••••

At last, the calm descends as evening shadows elongate the sidewalk.
A dog barks in the distance; train rumbles its disdain.
  The wind rests in the treetops and stares into the Buddha
  face of brother moon.
It's time to rest, time to renew, to reach for better days.

  Sunrise will change my mind.

YES, YOU WERE A CHALLENGE

Suspended animation….
Cinematography frames jammed in a reel – stopped in midair.
In fragments.
You passed me along the way – a blur.
Road Runner on his way to a painted tunnel.
I can follow you only in dreams.

Even the sunlight is silent.

•••••••••••••••
•••••••••••••••

You hold tight your emotions,
Give out passions in potions,
Then you find that sweet love's wine had soured.

So go back to your shelf
And play with yourself
Before you find out you're a coward.

PART II

AMBROGIO

The August night of 1973 was unusually hot and humid.

Longing for the lightest breeze to cool her body, she kicked off the down duvet. A droplet of sweat rolled off her forehead and onto her temple finally landing on the scented pillow where she lay her head. The sheer curtains on the window billowed softly in the almost nonexistent air as the moon, full and mysterious, lazily allowed the passing clouds to intermittently block its celestial views.

Shadows cast strange figures on the walls of the bedroom and even the cicadas, hidden from the rising heat, ceased their nightly concert.

She closed her eyes invoking Hypnos to abandon his fields of poppies but sleep, mischievous as an elf, eluded her blatantly sidestepping the portals of her consciousness.

Somewhere in the distance a wolf howled mournfully but his song did not startle her; on the contrary it felt like a lullaby, a comfort and homecoming.

A dreamlike state descended upon her light and silent as an owl in flight, and she felt herself slowly, blissfully falling into the arms of Morpheus.

A flutter of wings snapped her out of her reverie.

The room was dark now-the moon's face covered by the clouds.

The curtains hung motionless in front of the open window and a strange, shrill silence enveloped the night.

She saw him immediately: a dark, tall stranger standing motionless at the foot of her bed.

A fleeting thought passed through her that she should be frightened but mysteriously, she was not. On the contrary, she felt a strange comfort envelop her like a warm blanket on a cold night.

Watching him silently for what seemed a very long time she noted his slim body and dark hair that fell onto his shoulders. Even in the darkness of the room he appeared eerily handsome.

Lifting herself onto her elbows to get a better look she marveled at the fact that she felt neither fear nor alarm.

He seemed to float unencumbered by gravity as he slowly drew near her, and she welcomed him onto her bed. His arms were strong and muscular and he smelled vaguely of damp wood and earth, a strange combination she had not experienced before. His lips found hers and she yielded to a soft, sensuous and deep kiss as her body responded with the familiar flutter in her belly.

He kissed her ear, and she dug her nails into his back feeling the urgency to submit to this strange encounter.

Tracing a path from her ear and down her neck he lingered there, teasing her mercilessly.

Suddenly she felt a pressure and something warm trickled down her neck and onto the pillow.

She looked up to see him smile exposing blood-stained fangs and suddenly she was floating light as air, floating above the house, above the earth, above the clouds.

And then she realized that her life had taken a dark and uncompromising twist.

AMIR

The information I was given stated simply that my client was a 3-month-old baby with a birth defect that would terminate his life by the time he reached 8 months of age.

The family whose members were born in Afghanistan came to Canada from Pakistan several years before and settled in Brampton. The parents decided not to leave the baby in the hospital but to take him home and care for him themselves. As the child required 24 hour care the mother, whose name was Nazanin, kept watch through the day as well through the night leaving her on the edge of exhaustion and not allowing any time for the attention to the other child, four-year-old Farid. The baby boy named Amir lacked muscle strength and tone. He was not able to move his legs nor swallow. As a result, a naso-gastric tube was fed through his nostrils into his stomach in order to provide nourishment to his tiny body.

I wasn't sure of how well I would be received as I stood outside the home on the dreary fall day. As a hospice volunteer, my presence was always received with mixed emotions on the part of the of the clients' families. I was partly a deliverer of respite from the demands of the dying person and partly a messenger of death as the word "hospice" was a symbol of the finality of life.

Nazanin opened the door with little Amir in her arms. I introduced myself and she showed me into her living room. "Please make yourself at home; this is your home now." she said simply.

I felt the tension flow away. This was a warm and loving home.

We chatted for a while and I observed the baby boy whose laboured breathing came out in audible rasps and gasps.

"May I hold him?" I asked Nazanin.

A fleeting look of fear mingled with uncertainty alit on her face, but she held out the baby in my direction and, with all the confidence I could muster, I held the baby to my chest. Nazanin exhaled quietly and at that moment trust was born.

I visited the family once a week from that moment on allowing Nazanin to leave the house to take care of things that needed to be taken care of or spending some alone time with their 4-year-old son Farid.

One day when Nazanin went out Amir was particularly fussy. He squirmed and cried, his breathing coming in short gasps for air. I picked up his tiny limp body and carried him to the family room. The television was on tuned to the only channel available- Al Jazeera. I was grateful that the program airing was of a musician playing a setar. The music was soft and soulful. I sat down on the futon and held Amir close to my heart. The music played softly, and the sun's rays streamed through the window warming the room with its glow. I rocked slowly feeling love for this tiny suffering soul which privileged me with its presence if only for a short while.

Amir drew in a sharp breath. His breathing became regular and clear and he slept. I sat quietly for a very long time calming him with the beat of my heart, grateful for that moment in time which would stay in my memory for the rest of my days on earth.

Amir died in his mother's arms on December 26th of that year. I think of him and his loving family often.

Later in the Hospice newsletter appeared a quote from Nazanin:

"Margaret laid my son Amir's dying little body across her chest just like I would. She cradled him just like a mom and in that moment I knew I could trust her."

BUEN CABALLO

It was a perfect Cuban day when we arrived on the uninhabited island of Cayo Blanco via an old Russian Kamov helicopter. The flight was at best precarious as there were no doors on the wretched thing, and seatbelts were obviously not invented at the time of its creation. As we slid along its slippery benches, we watched the land below in horror and clutched the bars above for dear life. In the end it was all worth it as the snorkelling in the clear azure sea proved to be outstanding, and the beach as powdery and white as icing sugar.

Lunch was served in the forested area of the island on something that resembled a picnic table. The food was delicious, and we ate ravenously, washing it down with glasses of really bad Cuban wine which went down surprisingly easy, possibly due to the inhalation therapy of incredible sea air and the scent of pine mixed with smoke from the primitive barbeque. Residual terror from the helicopter ride and subsequent joy at having survived it, mixed with the appetite accelerator obtained through snorkelling, made the repast even more delightful.

The next adventure was to be a horseback ride in the forest.

There were five of us who signed up for this excursion and we eagerly anticipated the arrival of the cavalry. At last, five somewhat apathetic horses were led into the clearing where we waited. This made me ponder the moniker of "uninhabited" given to the island, and I was pretty sure that the horses did not arrive on the helicopter with us. Since I had ridden quite a bit in the past, the last thing I wanted is to plod along at a snail's pace while my "not so comfortable in the saddle" compatriots struggled to remain on top and not on the side or (oh horror) on the underside of their horses.

I sidled up slyly to the old guide who was in the process of assigning each horse to its rider and pushing a five dollar note into his grizzled hands whispered *Buen caballo, por favor.*

That was all the Spanish I knew other than *cuánto cuesta?* and *dónde está el baño?*, and I hoped that he would understand that I wanted a good horse and not him.

He sized me up for a moment and disappeared into the woods only to reappear momentarily leading a jet-black horse that danced and pranced like Pavlova on amphetamines. He handed me the reins and quietly said "El Diablo."

Oh Crap. My life flashed before my eyes. What did I get myself into? Now I had Satan himself to ride. Served me right.

I mounted this monstrosity wondering if I bit off more than I could chew, but El Diablo stood patiently and neighed quietly in approval.

Secure on the back of my fiery steed I sat and waited for the rest of the crew to be ready for our walk.

And waited…...

And waited…...

The old Cuban came up to me and pointed towards the small path which led into the forest.

"You go." he said in perfectly bad English.

"I go where?"

"You go." he said a little less politely pointing to the path.

The rest of the group was still figuring out which side of the horse to get up on, so the Cuban's directive was becoming very appealing. At this point the old man decided that he used up all the energy on words and just waved me towards the woodland path.

Oh well; no guts, no glory…. I turned Satan towards the path and nudged him gently. He responded quickly.

Hmmm…This could really be a "buen caballo", I thought.

Off we went. Slowly at first, and then seeing that the well-worn path seemed to go on and on, I squeezed El Diablo's side and clucked a universally recognized (by horses only) signal for let's get the heck out of here. And to my delight, that was what we did.

Trot turned to canter and then to a gallop. The group was left far behind and only the startled birds fluttered out of the trees as we flew by.

Suddenly the path ended and what I saw took my breath away. In front of us stretched miles and miles of untouched white beach and softly lapping waves of a turquoise sea. El Diablo snorted and lifted his head into the wind. He took a big breath in and I couldn't help but do the same. This was a picture from a novel, a painting of paradise and had there been a handsome man on a white stallion, every girl's dream.

I turned El Diablo to the right and we stood with our side to the ocean. Somehow, he knew what I was going to ask him, because he snorted and pawed the wet sand waiting for my command.

I did not make him wait. I squeezed his sides and clucked softly. That was all he needed, and we flew. The wind whipped through my hair and reddened my cheeks. El Diablo's hooves threw up a spray of salty water that glistened and shone with rainbow colours before it returned into the waiting arms of the sea. The beach seemed endless and as we galloped lost in our own rapture, I swear I could see the sprouting of wings on the black shimmering back of my horse.

My dark Pegasus.

How appropriate for my life.

I still think of my dark horse on those cold February days when aging bones ache with every humid day. All I have to do is close my eyes and we are flying once again, young, and free with wind in our hair/ mane, fans of sea spray landing on my thighs and El Diablo's joy electric and palpable.

DAVID

(BASED ON ACTUAL EVENTS)

He rolled down the window of the car and took a deep breath. The warm September air filled his lungs with the smell of pine trees that lined the miles of highway. He was on his way home.

The weekend at his sister's cottage in the Thousand Islands was just what he needed to regroup and regenerate after that knock- down -drag -out fight he had with David on Friday.

They had met 15 months ago in a gay bar in Toronto. He remembered the day like it was yesterday. He spotted David right away standing by the bar, chatting with a tall muscular blond guy. It was hard not to notice him; tall with jet black hair and those piercing amethyst blue eyes, he was the perfect front page of GQ magazine. Summoning up his courage, he walked up and introduced himself to the two men; a risky move at best, but it paid off. David smiled and invited him to have a drink with them. The big blond guy just snarled and walked away.

They spent the evening together and ended up at David's apartment on Wellesley Street in the heart of downtown. The sex was incredible. David was a skilled, considerable yet insatiable lover and that night they fell asleep exhausted and entwined in each other's arms.

Shortly afterwards, he moved into David's Wellesley Street apartment and they began the daily life as a couple in a city which was slowly accepting the emergence of the gay community as a separate and powerful entity. After all it was 1984!

Their life hummed along like any other city life, full of its challenges, its ups and its downs. The only fly in the ointment was David's extraordinary good looks which constantly attracted both male and female attention. And David did not discourage it. In fact, he sometimes sought it. And that was what caused the escalating disagreement on that Friday night in September when, frustrated and angry, he slammed the door of the apartment with the words "I'm outa here!" He called his sister from a phone booth outside to ask her if he could visit for a while.

Now he was on his way back. Back to the place he called his home. Back to the man who was his lover and his best friend. He tried to recall how the Friday argument began but could not. He laughed aloud realizing how we, as stupid human beings, could allow our emotions to ruin perfectly fixable moments in our lives. But he would fix that. He would buy a good bottle of wine on the way and apologize for the explosion. And that would be that. They would start again. They would find their way back to each other and to the vows they made together to live their lives in harmony and love.

He parked the car in the underground parking lot and walked- no, ran up the seven flights of stairs not to waste any time waiting for the elevator. Turning the key, he opened the door. The apartment was quiet. He noticed that the door of the coat closed was flung open and David's leather jacket was not there; he must have gone out. Oh well, he would wait with the wine and an apology. He would wait.

The kitchen looked unusually messy. There were dirty dishes in the sink –totally out of character for the very tidy David. On the table he noticed two cups of unfinished coffee. He found this odd and slightly disturbing. Did David have company on the weekend?

He walked towards the bedroom. The door was closed and there was a brown smear on the doorknob. He stood for a moment trying to take all this in. This was so out of character for what he grew to know about his partner. And as he stood there, he noticed a strange smell. He could not place it. It was reminiscent of the smell of rust, or of wet iron.

He turned the doorknob and walked in.

For a few moments he felt like he was in a dream. Nothing about this made any sense to him. The room was bathed in waning light which made the scene even more surreal. He never saw so much blood. Blood soaked the bed and dripped in rivulets onto the carpet where it lay in drying, rusty pools.

David lay naked and face down on the bed with his arms outstretched. Each wrist was fastened by leather strap to the iron post of the bed's headboard. His black hair was matted with blood, and his neck, back and buttocks covered in numerous slashes, barely visible under the smears and pools of clotting, drying blood. The handle of the kitchen knife buried in his back loomed ominously from under his left shoulder blade.

He stood transfixed by horror, still not processing the full extent of the scene, unable to move, unable to make a sound for fear of waking himself up from this nightmare, yet knowing that this was terribly real.

As senses returned to their normal function, his knees buckled and he vomited on the floor.

Slowly, he crawled out of the bedroom, picked up the phone receiver and dialed 911.

DREAMS

I dreamt of zebra skins: black stripes on white, white stripes on black. Bizarre images unfolded like a kaleidoscope in my head.

My dreams remind me of the "empty trash" function on my computer. Click on the icon, and the bar proceeds to move from zero to 100% until the bin is empty.

They seem silly to me these dreams, disjointed and full of imagery that would enthrall the most imaginative among us. Yet their function is profound for they take my hopes and fears and clean up the attic of my conscience by sweeping up the cobwebs and sweeping out the fragments of the broken bits.

Sometimes they dust off my hopes and prop them up in the middle of the room; sometimes they just clear out the trash bins and leave my hopes all covered in dust and waiting for another day.

I'm grateful for these scavenger dreams which nightly feast upon the unnecessary and unwanted scraps that occupy my heart and mind in the course of a daily journey. Grateful because they leave a space for the most human gift of all- hope; hope that springs eternal, albeit suppressed and re-directed.

It's somehow easier to carry on and plough through life for another day with the twinkling stars of hope on my epaulettes.

And so, we wait for tomorrow eagerly turning the pages of the calendar, searching for some inspiration…waiting, as Leonard Cohen aptly put it, "for a miracle to come."

We live, and work, and laugh and cry and love and take care of things, and in the quiet of the evening, by the light of the waning moon we wonder what the hell it's all about.

FOR MY DAUGHTER

You sleep with one tiny arm flung across your eyes – your lashes resting on your cheeks.

The bunny–the muchly kissed and often dragged around by the foot bunny lies alone flung to the foot of the bed.

The silence is unbearable.

It is broken only by the rhythm of your breathing and by the endless ticking of the clock.

You do not know that you carry the burden of my reason for survival.

You do not know that all around you there is hate, pain and suffering.

If I could only spare you all the grief…

If we could only go to where there is peace and love…. would that make you a worse person, or is suffering essential to strengthening of character?

I feel so alone sometimes that it makes me cry.

And immediately I feel ashamed because there are so many of those who are alone.

They stand in doorways, their faces blank with resignation.

They die on park benches in the cold of the winter.

They rummage through yellowed photographs on Christmas Eve.

They line up for a handout of hot soup at The Fred Victor Mission.

They clutch a bottle of cheap port, as if to draw strength from it…

But the silence sometimes….

FRIENDS

I walked to the beach alone at sunset. There was not a soul in sight. The tourists retired to their rooms to bathe and prepare their sunburned bodies for the evening ritual.

The beach welcomed me in silence.

And there, in the warm tropical air, the loneliness descended upon me like a cape and tears caught in my throat.

Suddenly and seemingly out of nowhere appeared a small black dog.

Her fur was matted with sand, her whiskers white with age and, visible on her throat was large, healed wound of battle or perhaps disease. She circled me in frenzied happiness and bounded down the beach suddenly plopping down in the sand and lying very still while she kept an eye on my approach.

As soon as I came near she started up her leaps and bounds only to run a little further. Then she lay down upon the sand to wait until I caught up. Delighted and amazed by her antics I turned and walked back towards the hotel. The little black dog turned also and overtook me with a joyful nip at the sandals I carried in my hand.

Playing and running as if to amuse me further she'd snap at the foamy waves that washed up on the shore. Her clowning made me laugh, the tears gone from my throat.

And so, we ran and played-two strangers on the turquoise border of the Cuban beach.

At last, hungry for the peace of the sunset I sat down in a chair facing the sea to watch the gold and orange streamers of the setting sun.

My newfound friend circled my chair and placed herself at my feet, ever watchful and wary of noises coming from the hotel, appointing herself the keeper of my safety. From time to time she put her paw on my lap asking for scratches behind her ear.

And so we sat-two creatures from two different worlds, momentarily coming together, touching in friendship, and parting forever when the moon came up.

FRIENDSHIP IS A SHELTERING TREE

- Samuel Taylor Coleridge

From the day we were born under the same sky on opposite sides of the globe we were different as night and day.

By the time we met, our lives still unfolding, we were set in our patterns.

I, a lion roaring at shadows fenced with real and imagined foes, rebelled at any standard blocking my path and bounded around corners at full speed in search of adventure.

You, a lamb, gentle by nature with stars in your eyes, yielded to traditions of your flock, yet managed to find a way to deftly sidestep orders to quietly have your way.

In your softness lay your strength. In my roar one could hear a note of bafflement.

You rocked weeping souls, bandaged earthly wounds and kept peace in the flock never revealing your breaking heart. At your expense, the world slept soundly.

I thrashed and fought my way out of the thorn bush that marked my boundaries, while you stayed well within the boundaries of yours.

You often found me lying there with paws full of thorns still roaring at life's injustices. Gingerly you removed them one by one and I grew to trust you more each day.

Soon I could find the comfort in the circle of your life and you, I suspect, could rest safe and protected within the circle of mine. No one would ever predict that our friendship would endure the ravages of time.

Years flew by with the speed of sound. Today we are wives, mothers, and grandmothers, yet we still dust off and unfurl the banners of our girlish dreams and run together in the gentle breezes of our friendship.

One day one of us will be left behind. Maybe soon and maybe in a few years, but before that joyous day when we are released from chains of this trial we will remain joined heart to heart by this golden thread knowing full well that when the night is cold and the world is unkind, we can seek solace in each other's voice which is so familiar and non-judgemental that it warms our naked souls in its quiet glow.

FRIGHT NIGHT

The clock on the kitchen wall tick-tocked tirelessly, its small hand inching towards 11:00 pm.

Steve sat at his computer finishing some business for the following day while Purrley, our cat lay on the mat in front of the patio door keeping a watchful eye on the back yard in case a wandering skunk or a racoon might deem it appropriate to conduct a midnight snoop.

I had retired to bed and was already in the magical land of dreams where Chanel purses grew on trees like low hanging fruit for the picking.

Suddenly, a strange, muffled sound caught Steve's ear. And it appeared that he was not the only one who heard it. Purrley sat straight up his blue eyes now black and big as saucers, and turned towards the basement door. The fur on his back stood up in a perfect ridge, giving him that certain punk-like appearance. The two of them temporarily froze, both staring at the closed door from behind which came this strange noise.For a moment all was quiet, and then they heard it again.

Slowly, Steve rose out of his chair and, scanning the kitchen for the nearest weapon, came up with a meat mallet which was drying in the dish rack. Purrley looked at him with disdain, but as he was occupied with the possibility of action, decided to let him get away with such a poor choice of a weapon.

Steve opened the door cautiously and waited.

Silence.

And then came a sound of a man's voice: "Heeeeeeelp me..."

Now let me tell you, dear reader, that in the event that it was I who found myself in this situation, I would have exploded like a Beaumark missile out of the house, barefoot and still wearing my flannel pajamas with the pink flying pigs and I would not have stopped running until I reached Quebec.

But not my two brave sentries. They skulked silently down the basement stairs; man and cat together.

"Heeeeeeelp me…"came the mournful cry. It was coming from the storage area of the furnace room. What to do? Oh what to do? Silence. And then "Heeeeeeelp me…"

Steve skulked up to the furnace room door and opened it cautiously, mallet poised for battle. The room was empty, except for several Rubbermaid containers, one of which tipped on its side. Out of this container came the mournful cry "Heeeeeeelp me…"

The result of Steve and Purrley's investigation would be recounted many times over family gatherings and dinners with friends.

Happy Halloween!

GOD'S SANDBOX

The phone rang shrilly in the modest Merzouga hotel room which I shared with my son. I looked at the clock beside my bed. Its green glowing face showed 3:45am. We knew that this was going to happen, but in the darkness we both wondered what in the name of heaven possessed us to do this to ourselves.

Travelling through Morocco had been a dream of mine and I wanted to share it with my son Adrian in whom I instilled the same passion for travel as my own.

We quickly got out of our beds. No need to dress as we didn't fully undress the night before anticipating a swift morning departure. The night was dark and surprisingly cool-cool enough for a windbreaker.

Two 4x4s vehicles stood in readiness at the front of the hotel as we, and the other four weary travellers with whom we were sharing this adventure, stumbled bleary eyed out of our rooms. Our guide waited patiently until we slumped into the vehicles and amid futile dreams of hot coffee and a warm bed, were off.

Jostled around in the most uncomfortable of conditions we reached a small caravan waiting for us at the edge of the desert. Six fine camels lay in a row while two Touareg handlers in indigo blue tagelmusts led us to their beasts. I was already familiar with my camel from a previous trek. His name was Mamoun, which meant "trustworthy". He was light beige in colour reminding me of cafe au lait which I craved more and more as the night unfolded. His hide was much paler than the other camels and this made him more valuable, or so claimed his handler.

Mamoun lay quietly in the sand with his legs tucked neatly underneath. Occasionally he chewed his cud rotating his lower lip from right to left and then reversing the process. He was gentle and patient and by now I knew that he liked scratches behind the ears. I stroked his muzzle and rubbed his ear. He quietly bleated his approval, his long lashes blinking slowly as he revelled in this welcome show of affection.

We were getting ready to mount our camels so I swung my feet across Mamoun's back and settled into the cushioned leather saddle. I knew what came next. It would be what I called the weeble wobble, and I firmly grabbed the horn in the front of the saddle in anticipation.

Camels rise up by extending their necks and kneeling on their front legs, a motion which pitches the rider backwards. Then the back legs straighten, which in turn pitches the rider forward. Finally they rise from the kneeling position which slightly wobbles the rider forward and then backwards until balance is restored. (The first time I rode a camel was in 1970 and I wore a miniskirt. Don't ask…) No matter, we were up and ready to go.

Camels share a strange way of walking with two other animals: the cat and the giraffe. They move both legs on one side, and then both legs on the other side. This gives them a swaying, rocking motion which can make a novice rider feel queasy, and thus gives them the name Ships of the Desert.

This swaying motion however had a soothing effect on me, and I had to stop myself from falling fast asleep which would result in a tumble from a height of seven feet or so, make me a fine spectacle and a provide few moments of entertainment for my half-asleep compatriots.

After what seemed like several hours which turned out to be only 20 minutes, we reached the end of our caravan.

Before us rose the Erg Chebbi dunes of the Moroccan Sahara and in the darkness of the star splashed sky they loomed ominously like a scene from a science fiction movie. Our camels stopped and proceeded to lie down in a reverse weeble wobble.

In the cold darkness with millions of stars serving as our only light we stood transfixed at the foot of the dune which reached towards the sky at a height of 80 feet or so. This was to be our climb.

Awkwardly, we began the ascent in a single, weary file, our shoes sinking into the dark sand which made the trek even more difficult. Someone came up with the idea of taking our shoes off and we did so enjoying the coolness and the deceptive moisture of the dune. Our guides remained with the camels below so they could not warn us of the sleeping scorpions underneath the sand. Luckily none of us desert newbies stepped on or upset any of these snoozing, bad tempered beasts.

Eventually, in the darkness, we reached the summit and stood on the crest of the dune in complete exhausted silence.

Slowly, almost imperceptibly as if guided by some divine signal, a thin band of pale light appeared on the horizon. One by one we sat down on the cool sand facing this long golden ribbon and watched as it grew and thickened and flooded the desert with orange light.

Behind us, the dune revealed its sharp crest and the perfectly sculptured ripples which decorated its face; a divine masterpiece created by the wind. Other than our footprints on one side it was pristine, mysterious and untouched.

The silence around us was almost shrill.

Far off a Bedouin tent appeared flooded with the morning light. In front of it lay three camels. A donkey tethered to a pole stood waiting patiently to begin the day's chores.

The dunes of Erg Chebbi cast surreal shadows upon the face of the waking Sahara and every one of us in this small group, feeling like a human speck, transfixed by the vastness and the glory of the spectacle before us, would carry home this ethereal, spiritual, and strangely altering memory of sharing this one magical moment of a sunrise in the Sahara.

THE STAGES OF GRIEF

DESPAIR
Breath coming in short, ragged and shallow gasps for air.
Chest bound tightly by and invisible steel band.
Throat constricted-each swallow causing pain.
Eyes seeing colours muted, sounds coming to the ears through a heavy dark curtain.
Tears springing to the eyes, flowing in endless streams onto my hands.
That evening, driving alone with the sunroof open on a dark country road, I found myself howling, wailing, and swept away by wave after wave of true unbridled despair.
The star splashed sky, the pine trees all around me, and the only sign of human intrusion being the two-lane highway underneath my wheels, gave me their blessing to grieve so unashamedly.

ANGER
Steel core, white hot with fire rising high and higher, consuming all breathable oxygen, gurgling inside like lava, gaseous explosion imminent. An ancient, colossal cauldron preparing a deadly feast.
Steam hiss under a cap, bulging with pressure, its searing power held thinly, temporarily.
A merciless crash of house high waves against the bow of a mighty ship. Boards creaking. Masts tumbling. The sea's unrelenting rage splintering the ship as sacrifice.
Resounding slap against a cheek, a prelude to a blade sunk into flesh for twenty seventh time. Red lights exploding all around. The smell of iron stronger than the silence of escaped life.
Gouging, clawing, tearing, irrational, irreparable anger.

ACCEPTANCE
Eventually empty and spent, I set out to prepare myself for numbness.

The healing, impersonal distancing. The uninvolved spectatorship.

I looked at colours and saw them flat and empty. My glazed, drug-like stare found everything unimportant, nothing amusing not touching, nor tragic.

Merely observing, devoid of feeling. The ultimate success.

JOY

The pain takes my breath away; it has been fifteen hours of this unrelenting suffering. Now I just want it to stop.

"Push". The doctor grumpily gives a boot-camp order.

Monumental effort and a squeal comes from my nether regions.

I hear laughter.

"He peed on the doctor, the little rascal!" the nurse tells me.

They bring me a somewhat cleaned up and swaddled bundle which just moments ago lived inside me.

His squished face shows red marks from the forceps and he regards me with dark blue eyes. Perfect, tiny fingers grasp my hand.

A lava of overwhelming love rises in me from my feet to the top of my head.

My baby. My son, Adrian.

Joy

~~~~~~~~~~

The moment I start my motorcycle, the heavens open up.

I am 53 years old and I am taking my "MX" exit exam to get a motorcycle license. The earpiece is in and the examiners are in the car behind me; they will give me instructions as they monitor my progress.

The rain is relentless but there is no choice. This is life, and on a bike one will encounter such challenges.

I carry out their orders although the sound in the earpiece is not good. Approaching the highway, I merge into traffic quickly and safely. The rain is washing over the face shield of my helmet and it is hard to see.

I'm sure I have failed the test; this is just too difficult.

We return to the starting point. I stop the bike and get off disheartened.

"Congratulations!" the examiners exclaim handing me a certificate.

I have 90 kilometers to ride to reach home and it is still pouring.

The certificate is tucked inside my leather jacket which is now covered by my rain gear.

On highway 9,the drivers give me a "thumbs-up" from the dry comfort of their cars.

I am beside myself with happiness.

Joy

~~~~~~~~~~

It is a hot and muggy summer day.

I am wearing a tee shirt with "Big Ass Toys Are Not Just for Boys" on the back.

1200 cc's of Harley Davidson engine respond to the twist of my throttle.

The country road is winding and empty. The scent of pine in the surrounding forest washes over me as the sun beats down. The wind whips my face as I ride alone.

This is paradise.

Joy

~~~~~~~~~~

We are in the area of Thailand that is very close to the "Golden Triangle" where Thailand, Burma and Laos meet.

There are four of us and we are sitting on plastic cushions on the floor of a "long-tail" boat which is heading up the Kok river to the Dusit Island hotel in Chiang Rai. Our guide and the boat operator have us in their care.

It is the middle of the dry season and the water level on the river is very low.

Suddenly, we are stuck.

Rolling up our pant legs we get out of the boat and begin to push it off the sandbar.

It won't budge.

The giggles overtake us and float on the wind down the river.

Another long-tail boat passes us safely and its laughing occupants give us the thumbs-up.

We are wet and sweating from the unrelenting heat of the Thai dry season and we are having the time of our lives.

Joy

~~~~~~~~~~

The dinner at the lovely, tiny restaurant was magnificent as always, and my husband and I are about to head home. We are in downtown Brampton and it is December-the time when lights of every colour and type paint the city core and delight the eye.

Gage Park is quiet and magical in the glow of the colourful bulbs. The tree trunks are wrapped in lights; they seem to float unencumbered in the air.

The beauty overwhelms us.

Joy

~~~~~~~~~~

There is music and laughter. The crib is set up in the middle of the living room and our babies play happily in it. The dogs joyfully meet and greet everyone who comes in as Christmas Carols fill the air.

The table is set with twelve traditional dishes and there is one extra chair for the "unexpected visitor".

It will remain empty for the duration of the evening.

Sharing the thin, wafery "host" we wish each other good things in the coming year.

We are together, we are healthy, and we are alive.

It is Christmas,1978

Joy

~~~~~~~~~~

LESSONS IN LIFE

Among the choices that we are allowed to make, some directions of our personal paths are pre-destined.

When times get ugly and tough, those are opportunities for lessons learned. Take the lesson and turn it into integrity and experience.

When times are good, revel in them. Keep their memory for later; it will sustain you when clouds gather.

There is nothing that you cannot do if you put your mind to it.

Seek the environment that brings out the best in you.

Don't dwell on your losses

Take what you can from life but do it responsibly: do not hurt any living being, keep the environment as pure as you can.

Don't be afraid of any of your dreams no matter how unattainable they may seem at the moment.

Go for it.

Learn from bad situations; let them build your strength because you will have to take under your wings those who are still weak.

Laugh a lot; find humour in everyday things.

Don't give up. If a situation overwhelms you, take a break and walk away-for the moment. Come back and try again; until you succeed. And in most cases, you will succeed.

Practice random acts of kindness at least once a day, no matter how small.

Refrain from judgement or pity; you don't know what Karmic debt someone is paying.

Keep the empathy. Send thoughts of love to the oppressed, the wounded, and the struggling.

Take a day off to feel sorry for yourself if things get too tough; but only a day at the most. Dust yourself off, shake it off and begin anew next day.

Things always seem harder at the end of the day and ever harder in the middle of the night. Tell yourself that you will think about it tomorrow; return to handle the problem refreshed and revitalized.

Prioritize; put most important things on the "to–do" list at the front and do them. Forget the others but only until you finish what is first to be done. Like dominoes, everything else will take its rightful place and will be easier to manage.

Take time for yourself; if you are not strong, you cannot be of any help to those who need it.

Recognize that "these ARE the good old days" and honour the moment.

Travel. See other places and meet people from all corners of the earth. You will see how alike we all are in spite of our cultural backgrounds.

Do something that pushes your boundaries. This will teach you to overcome doubt and fear.

Always be decent even when others are not.

Forgive. Do not let anger and desire for revenge eat you alive like acid from the inside out. Let go and you will find peace.

Remember that you will attract what you project. Be kind and kindness will find you every time.

When you give, do not do it with any expectation of recognition or thanks. Give for the pure right to be able to give.

If you have beseeched, prayed, begged, and bargained with the Higher Power and still do not get your wish, yield to the process. You will see later that sometimes the greatest gift is to be denied what you wished for.

If you cannot be thankful for what you receive, be happy for what you escape.

MICHNIÓW

"I have a surprise for you" he said. "I'm going to take you back in time."

I was visiting Poland, the country of my birth. The year was 1999. Janusz was my childhood friend and later the love of my young life. Our parents met when I was 3 and he was 4 and according to my mom, we were engaged by the time I was 5.

I left Poland at the age of 10 and Janusz told me many years later that he cried for days not understanding why they took me away.

Our paths crossed again when I came to Poland in 1970. By now he was engaged, and I was a frivolous young Canadian travelling around Europe on my own. Our brief encounter cemented our deep connection, but any plans of togetherness were not to come to fruition. Having completed school, he was scheduled for a compulsory stint in the army. Leaving communist Poland was not an option. For me staying in the country which was under the communist rule, away from my family and the life to which I was now accustomed was not in the cards either.

"Where are you taking me?" I asked, curiosity getting the better of me.

"You'll see."

We drove out of the city of Warsaw, leaving the hustle and bustle behind. The roads turned from four- lane highways to two lanes and then to country roads. And then I saw the sign. "Michniów".

My heart rose into my throat for a few seconds. I looked at him in disbelief. This was the little village at the foot of the Świętokrzyskie Mountains where our parents brought us every summer. For two months we stayed with a farm family in their home. Janusz and his family stayed a few houses down.

The family we lived with consisted of a mother, a father, and a young boy of 10 years of age or so. The house was a modest hut with no electricity or running water. There was a well in the back and an outhouse further away. The outhouse terrified me and actually contributed to my obsessive arachnophobia. It was dark in there and every corner was occupied by a veritable cornucopia of spiders and their clever webs. I was terrified to take down my pants and sit on the hole which served as a toilet for fear that those monster spiders which resided behind me would take that very opportunity to explode from their webs onto my bare bum and sink their monster teeth into my nether regions.

The barn was a fantastic playground. Filled with hay to the very top, it served as a sort of Chucky Cheese's recreation center where we could climb up a couple of tiers and throw ourselves into the mountain of hay squealing and giggling until the farmer came in and put an end to the mayhem we caused.

Two cows lived in the shed behind the house-a mother and a daughter. They both had horns and we had to be very careful especially around the younger cow. That one exhibited a certain annoyance with anyone under the age of 30 and often tried to spear us with her still growing horns. The older cow was much, much more laid back and she's the one I learned to milk-a feat much more difficult than one can imagine. The payoff was a metal cup full of frothy, warm, richly creamy milk that I would gulp down with sheer pleasure.

The farmer had two horses and a wagon that resembled an elongated "V" for carrying hay. Some days he would let us go with him into town. We bounced around the carriage like ping pong balls and yelped with delight as he urged his horses on with soft whistles and light whip of the reins.

The farmer's wife baked bread and churned sweet butter from the milk of the two cows. I still remember the smell of baking bread and the long-abandoned taste of its slices spread with a thick layer of fresh butter.

At night, my grandmother lit the naphthalene lanterns on the little table in our bedroom and I, tucked in and enveloped by down pillows and comforters, filled my nostrils with that strange familiar scent while she read me a bedtime story.

Days were full of with discovery as Janusz and I wandered off into the fields and forests in search of adventure. We waded barefoot in streams watching the tadpoles as they swam, their long tails wiggling back and forth propelling them on. Sometimes we would catch them and bring them home in a jar wishing to keep them as pets until they turned into full grown and magic frogs. My grandmother had none of it and ordered us to release them back to the stream, telling us of the weeping frog mothers and fathers searching for their babies. This horrified us so much that we ran back with our jar and let the tadpoles swim away with visions of their subsequent and joyful family reunions in our heads.

Then there were anthills to observe. The busy traffic around an anthill was a constant source of fascination and discovery. We could never upset their houses. That would be unfair.

While in the forest, we used the huge rock formations which lived among the trees as shelters from the imagined enemy soldiers just like we heard the partisans did in the real struggle for survival.

When we got hungry during our day at play there was plenty to eat. We picked red raspberries often scratching our arms on the thorny bushes. There were plump blueberries that dyed our fingers indigo and dark juicy plums hanging low on the branches. If we felt particularly energetic we could pull hazelnuts off the trees and break their shells with stones to reach the delicious nuts inside. Gooseberries, lingonberries, even tiny wild strawberries were often on our menu.

Sometimes the overindulgence of these gifts of the land led to an upset tummy and you guessed it, to a visit of the dreaded spider emporium behind the house.

The carefree days of our childhood summers filled with wonder, laughter and love passed quickly leaving a sweet memory of sunshine, green fields, fragrant forests, and clear, clean streams.

Now, many decades later we stood at the edge of the very forest which we left behind so many years ago. The rock formations still stood silent and proud, keeping the secrets of the days gone by.

I could not find the farmers' house we stayed in. The village looked so much…newer. So much less…pure.

My eyes filled with tears for which I could not find an explanation, and as I turned to Janusz I saw behind him a group of large brown wooden crosses.

"I don't remember them," I whispered.

"They weren't there when you left," he said.

"Why are they here?"

"You don't know the history of this town?" He seemed surprised.

The only history of this town I knew was my own.

And then he told me the story.

*Under the Nazi occupation, the village of Michniów was one of centres of the Polish underground partisan movement. On 12 and 13 July 1943, a population of Michniów was massacred by the German Police units (of the 17th and the 22nd Police Regiments), commanded by Hauptmann Geruf Mayer, for helping the partisans.

After the first massacre on 12 July, when 98 men were burned alive in barns, the partisans headed by Jan Piwnik "Ponury", made a retaliatory assault on a train from Kraków to Warsaw at night. On the next day, the Germans returned to continue the massacre. During a period of two days, at least 204 inhabitants were killed - 103 males, 53 women and 48 children.

A further 11 persons - the only ones suspected by the Germans for underground activities - were sent to Auschwitz concentration camp, where 6 died. The village was completely burned to the ground.*

So, this is why our parents brought us here. My mother lived and fought in the forests and side by side with the partisans during the war. She must have known what happened in Michniów. She brought me here to show me how beautiful the peaceful land can be and maybe to heal some of those awful memories that lived in her mind's eye.

Today when I watch television and see children play in sad and troubled places ravaged by conflict and war I feel blessed that in some way I was protected and allowed to run and dream and know that I was safe.

References:

1. "Central Statistical Office (GUS) - TERYT (National Register of Territorial Land Apportionment Journal)" (in Polish). 2008-06-01.

2. (Polish) Michnów at Muzeum Wsi Kieleckiej

3. Bogdan Hildebrandt (in Polish), Partyzantka na Kielecczyźnie 1939-1945, Wydawnictwo MON, Warsaw 1970, p. 173-174

* (Polish) Michnów at Muzeum Wsi Kieleckiej (Kielce Region Countryside Museum) page [retrieved 19-7-2010]

NUMBER 77

It was with a heavy heart that I set out to Oakville Trafalgar hospital to undergo a diagnostic procedure. My heart was heavy for a couple of reasons: the first, obvious one, that I didn't know the cause of my distress, and the second that I had spent 40 years working in several hospitals and had the unfortunate experience of seeing what really goes on behind the curtain.

So I trudged, dragging my feet down the grim corridors which sported the tired look of having too many feet trudge and drag along their floors, towards the sign that said Nuclear Medicine.

I slithered into the waiting room. Much to my delight there were only four people sitting silently in the chairs: two women who appeared to be a mother and a daughter, a man lost in a newspaper perusal, and a girl of maybe eighteen or so with eyes fixed on the TV suspended from the ceiling in the corner of the room.

Clutching my requisition I walked up to the receptionist. She was a woman of about 50 with a round face that hosted considerable jowls any English Bulldog would be proud to own, tiny eyes the colour of a neglected pond peering out from behind tiny bi-focals and short bits of straw-like hair that stuck out in the direction of all four compass points.

As she offered no greeting of any sort, I extended my hand with the requisition. Before I could utter any sound she growled: "Take a number and sit down."

I looked around slightly astonished at the fact that I had to take a number, since there was no one else in line but rules are rules and, as an occasional rule follower I thought it best to do what I was told. I extracted a number from the red number machine in front of the receptionist and pulled out number 75 - as good a number as any.

Clutching this ticket to the next step, I obediently walked to the chairs at the back of the waiting room and lowered myself onto the one I chose as my place of rest. Before my hind quarters could hit the seat,

I heard the familiar hiss: "Number seventy five."

I temporarily froze in mid-air paralyzed by the absurdity of this situation, but recovered in time to redeem my faculties and move forward once again towards the happy receptionist. She extended her hand and for a moment I entertained the idea of shaking it, but thought better of it in view of her obviously absent sense of both decorum and humour.

She perused my requisition and tisked disapprovingly.

"You have to go to the X-Ray Department to check in.

"But I am having a Nuclear Medicine scan, and this is the ….."

She speared me with her pond scum eyes. "You were booked in X-Ray and you have to go there." She spoke slowly as one would when one is ready to pull the trigger and the victim is nothing less than a borderline idiot.

I wasn't going to debate the point. I took my documents and exited -stage left.

About twenty feet to the left of Nuclear Medicine was the X-Ray reception. Two receptionists sat behind glass which I concluded must have been installed as bulletproof. I walked up to one of the women, and she looked up from her very important paper shuffling long enough to say: "Go behind the red line."

I looked around. Behind me in all its lonely glory was the red line. I stood obediently behind it.

"Next." I heard.

By now I was getting giddy. This was partly due to the fact that I had not eaten anything since the evening before but more to the point, because I now felt that I had entered some altered dimension where all rules in the book of medical reception will have the hungry, exhausted and pain riddled patient dancing to any tune the empowered employees deem appropriate at the moment.

She looked at my papers, took my Health Card and announced in a triumphant voice: "Now go back to Nuclear Medicine and check in with them."

Back I went.

I determined that I would not be caught disregarding the stern and inflexible rules of the uber-receptionist who ruled nuclear Medicine. I pulled Number 76. Yes, I was still the only one requiring attention. This time my gluteus maximus (actually glutei maximi, as both of them hit the chair at the same time) had time to lower itself completely and sink into the plastic chair.

"Number 76",I heard.

Happy that this was proceeding so smoothly I jumped up and gleefully handed her the number and my file.

"Oh, you don't need a number and you don't need to give these papers to me. Just sit down." Her thin lips tightened forming a horseshoe pattern and making her jowls quiver in disgust.

By now my giddy personality was morphing into something much darker, but the knowledge that I needed this department more than it needed me was keeping me in check. I sat down and began the seemingly unending process of the getting to know the hospital waiting room better than your own back yard.

By now the straw haired troll from hell had turned her back towards the reception area and immersed herself in a conversation with a woman who perched on the counter behind the glass.

An older man stumbled in tripping over the small rug at the entrance. For a moment I thought that I had to spring forward out of my chair in order to prevent him from performing an Olympic quality face plant which would require that he wait for and undergo even more diagnostic tests than he originally came for, but he caught his balance and proceeded towards the magic red number-spitting machine. After pulling out a number he obediently and silently came back to the row of seats where I sat and rested there clutching the paper which I was pretty sure was number 77.

The receptionist sat with her back to the room, and with her new friend sipped coffee and exchanged gossip. Nobody paid attention to the old man and his number 77.

The technologist bounced into the reception area like Tigger on a good day and called my name. I followed her into the room losing sight of the old man.

I'm pretty sure that he is still sitting there covered in cobwebs, teetering on the edge of his faux leatherette chair, weak with hunger and saddened by the lack of human contact. He waits to hear those longed for words: "Number 77!"

PUŁAWSKA 41

I was in Warsaw with my mother who persuaded me to accompany her in returning to the place of our birth; a place we left in 1959 after subtle but troubling persecution of my mother by the KGB for her activities in the Polish Home Army, which doggedly but in the end futilely resisted the takeover by the communist regime at the end of World War Two.

My cousin Teresa and I were just returning from the theatre when I realized that we were in the neighbourhood where I grew up and just steps away from the house we lived in until our departure for Canada.

"Come, let's take a better look". Teresa steered me towards the low-rise apartment building.

As we approached a weird feeling came over me-like this was a dream- like I would find the scenes of my childhood playing themselves out any minute.

The small garden where I played with the children appeared intact and as I looked up I saw the windows of our apartment.

Now I was seven years old.

Teresa opened the heavy gate of the building and I walked into the foyer.

The old mailbox was still there, and the stairs down which I fell as a small child leaving me with a tiny scar above my eyebrow stood silent in the waning light of day.

These stairs led up to the first landing; on the left side was our door, and behind it was my grandmother with supper ready and waiting for me.

A feeling of a moment frozen in time gripped my heart and ghosts danced on the stairs and in the hallway.

It was all I could do not to burst into tears.

I had a dream last year, and it was of this moment.

It was dark, just like tonight, and everything I saw in the dream looked the same in real life.

Even the stores across the street were the same.

This old apartment stood as a silent testament to my family's life: from the outbreak of war, my grandmother's quiet conspiracy headquarters, my cousin's bravery, my mom's arrest, nocturnal visits of the Gestapo and later, the KGB, the tragedies, joys, births, deaths, laughter, tears, wins and losses, the shadows on my bedroom wall cast by the passing streetcars, the rumble of the communist tanks on the street below, my piano lessons, dark school morning fortified with hot oatmeal, my grandmother's loving hands combing my hair, stroking my face, drying my tears.

It all came back to me like a sea of molten lava and covered me completely.

I stood at the bus stop and shook and shook like a leaf.

I could not calm down; I could not get a grip-not for a long, long time.

SCHOOL DAYS

I was born in Warsaw, Poland three years after the end of World War ll.

Our apartment on the second floor overlooked the busy Puławska Street with its streetcar tracks, shops and sidewalks always teeming with pedestrians.

At night, the shadows of passing streetcars rolled across the small bedroom which I shared with my grandmother. It became somewhat of a comfort to hear their rumble and watch their shadows slide across the wall.

I don't remember much of my earliest years; only what I saw in faded photographs, but I have a vague recollection of being sheltered and well loved by both my mother and my grandmother.

My biological father was absent, and my stepfather joined the family when I turned two. For many years I believed that he was my true daddy as this was my mother's wish.

When I turned seven, the age all children in Poland began grade school, it was time to enter into the educational system.

My mother was a firm believer that a young lady must not only be well mannered and well educated but she also that must be able to play a musical instrument. This was a throwback to her own upbringing as dictated by the privileged society in which she grew up.

Thus began the search for a choice of instrument.

Having a soft spot in her heart for the music of a violin, my mother decided that this would be the direction in which I was to go.

My opinion in this matter actually never even came into play; as I think about this, my opinions were never called upon as I was a child and my role was to obey.

Sadly, fate reared its imposing head in the form of my pinky fingers. They were slightly crooked- a congenital gift bestowed upon my person by whatever entity was in charge of putting me together. This imperfection immediately ruled out the violin as it meant that I would have a hell of a time trying to reach those tricky strings with my bowed pinkies.

On to choice number two: the mighty piano, where even with the altered shape of my fingers I could still reach the keys and produce hopefully dulcit tones to delight the ear. Hopefully. Maybe one day.

With that thought in mind my mother enrolled me in the Fryderyk Chopin Music School in the heart of the old city on Miodowa Street. I began the daunting task of first, getting there on the public transit and second of finding my niche among the students already familiar with the surroundings.

School day mornings eventually followed their own routine: out of bed, wash, eat breakfast of oatmeal or Cream of Wheat and endure the torment of having my hair combed and braided. "Why the torment?" you might ask.

By the time I was seven years old my hair never having been cut, reached to my mid-calf. Every day my grandmother would comb the thick tresses starting at the bottom and working her way up. Doing this in reverse was almost impossible as the tangles would not yield as easily, and the experience would be even more painful.

My grandmother was a gentle and a patient woman and I much preferred it when she combed out my hair to the time my mother would get a hold of me. That experience was definitely a dreaded one as my mother was always in a hurry, even when she didn't need to be, and tugged at the tangles ordering them to yield instead of using the gentle prodding which was my grandmother's modus operandi.

With the morning routine completed, it was time to go to the bus stop which was just outside our apartment.

There, my grandmother waited for the bus with me and seeing me safely off returned home.

Alone with my backpack I travelled quite a distance to the other side of Warsaw where I alit in the old town square and walked for another block or so to Miodowa Street. There, behind imposing iron gates stood my music school.

On the way I always passed a couple of bombed out buildings still in disrepair since the war. It never ceased to amuse me how I could see their rooms with the colourful walls exposed to the street. For me, the best was a bathroom with a claw foot bath standing proudly on display as if waiting for its occupant to come in with a bathrobe and a newspaper to read while soaking in the warm water.

There was also the occasional cross and a plaque on a fence or a building with a number of civilians gathered at that spot and shot by the German Gestapo.

All this was what was familiar and strangely normal in my life. I didn't know anything else.

The school was in an older building. It had white walls and very shiny hardwood floors polished to a mirror like sheen. All the children had to bring slippers which they changed into before entering the pristine hallowed hallways; the very hallways which would give us the idea of "the snake'

This was a game we would play at recess. We formed a long chain by holding each others' hands. Once in position, we ran as fast as we could in the huge hallway suddenly changing direction. Everyone would take his or her turn at the very end of the chain and as the "snake" began to turn he or she would stop running and pulled by the rest of the children, would slide at break-neck speed while squealing with delight.

I don't remember why we weren't stopped and reprimanded by the staff, but I remember the thrill in my chest as I slid in continuous arcs at the end of the tail of my school days' "snake".

But not all was carefree and fun.

The library was my favourite place and, as an avid bookworm, I could spend happy moments picking out the next book to lose myself in. It was also a quiet place and it drew me in time after time.

We also had to wear uniforms. Those consisted of a dress-like overall which buttoned down the front and fit over the street clothes. It was navy blue with a white collar, and it removed any trace of individuality other than hair and facial features. To this day I blame my penchant for a "clothes-horse" behaviour on the days of this restricted habit.

Few times in the school-year came the dreaded exams. The addition of the music exam was an unwelcome event and it went like this:

The auditorium was designated to be the place where music exams took place.

I sat on a large bench with several of my colleagues outside the seven-foot-tall mahogany doors which led to this dreaded room.

When my name was called, I approached it with rubbery legs and entered. There at the long wooden table at the back of the room sat a panel of judges which might as well have been a combination of ogres and witches for the fear they instilled in my young heart.

At the other end of the seemingly endless and echoing room stood a Steinway grand piano with a mercifully adjustable bench which I always had to alter in order to reach the keys and at the same time be able to reach the pedals.

With my teeth chattering and my heart pounding like the entire corps of Kodo Drummers I climbed up on the bench and, organizing my thoughts, began to play from memory assorted works of Chopin, Bach, Shubert and Haydn, which I had practiced every day for weeks.

As I played the nervousness dissipated and I lost myself in the familiar chords and trills of the music which filled the room.

Once I finished my repertoire I descended from the bench, curtsied and happily left the room.

I never failed these exams even though I was sure every time that I would.

Much later in life knee-buckling experience revisited me when I played at the Kiwanis festival and at the Royal Conservatory of Music in Toronto, although the Steinway seemed a lot smaller than I remembered!

At the age of ten I left my school of Music for good to begin a new life with my family in Canada.

It was an experience filled with fear, trepidation, excitement and tears as I slowly learned the language and began to assimilate into the society so different from the one I knew.

I think about those lost days sometimes and how they served to enrich this journey that would be my life.

"SOMETIMES I SITS AND THINKS, AND SOMETIMES I JUST SITS..."

The warm and sunny August day reluctantly gave way to the approaching evening.

One cloud, shaped like an eagle in flight, glowed with the waning orange light of the setting sun.

My husband and I sat on the deck enjoying after dinner liqueurs having finished our al fresco dinner.

We sat in silence.

Our silence was not a result of nothing left to say nor was it due to an argument. It simply was.

That's all.

A mourning dove flew down from the rooftop making its strange whistling sound, and sat on the edge of the birdbath.

The resident bunny, suspected of setting up house behind the shed in the back of the garden, sat up straight in the middle of the lawn with ears stiff as little antennas, ready to hop away should unexpected turn of events herald impending doom.

A lone bat flew overhead silent and focussed- its radar, a wonder of ancient technology setting its course across the sky.

Crickets tuned their instruments before their evening symphony would delight the ear of willing patrons.

The lilies in the bouquet adorning the patio table willingly released their sweet lily scent which floated like dandelion puffs across the yard.

Somewhere in the distance a train rumbled its protest at having to carry such a heavy load on such a glorious summer night.

We sat in silence lost in the sounds, the scents, the sights of this amazing summer day, knowing that although there may be many more summer days, this one, this very one was unique.

This one would never grace us with its presence again.

I used to wonder why the old folks would sit on park benches with nothing to do.

Now, in the waning golden light I knew.

THAILAND

I was on a ferry that sailed from Phuket to a lovely remote island on the Andaman Sea. There were only one or two tourists on the boat other than me. The rest of the passengers were local Thai people looking forward to a picnic and some great swimming on the coral reef.

At sunset, after a grand day of snorkeling and relaxing, as we were preparing to leave the island, we had to climb into a small rowboat ready to take us to a waiting ferry moored a few hundred feet away from the shore.

Quickly settled on the small bench in the rowboat, I watched the people piling in. A woman holding a baby was trying to keep her balance as she stepped into the swaying boat. Without hesitation I extended my arms to take the child from the mother who quickly passed the little girl to me.

The child was dressed in a pure white dress and on her head, a frilly white bonnet tried to contain a shock of black hair escaping from beneath its rim.

The baby girl looked at me with big black almond eyes and smiled. She was so cute that I couldn't help myself and, in that way familiar to all mothers since time immemorial, I began to rock and coo and hum a song long forgotten; a song that I sang while holding my own children to my heart many, many years before.

The boat began to move. The mother did not approach me to retrieve her child but instead chattered with her friends, not even glancing in my direction, appearing to completely ignore me.

"What am I, a damn babysitter?" raced through my mind. "She didn't even say 'Thank You.'" And with that internal conversation, I began to feel more and more angry.

When we reached the ferry, the mother turned and looked into my eyes, smiling. I handed the child to her and at that very moment, like a stream of light, a kind of realization enveloped me.

It was a great gift that the mother had given me.

Seeing my delight, she handed me her jewel, and by turning away her eyes she saved me from embarrassment so that I could freely delight in my interaction with the baby.

It was she who was doing me a favour.

And at that moment I knew that the more distant the tradition, the more profound the lesson.

Thailand continued to serve me lessons in the following days and weeks which, from that moment on, did not go unnoticed and I wrote about it as follows:

Everywhere I go here I feel the comforting presence of someone or something very protective. A great peace descends upon me as heavy as the scent of jasmine around my neck.

Peace - from the tinkling of the brass bells on the roof of the chedi, to the stillness in the "second path" in the monks' quarters.

From the dark, star-lit nights in the north with the mist that rises off the rice paddies in the morning, to the kaleidoscope of the coral reefs in the Andaman Sea in the south.

From the early morning crow of the roosters to the steady roll of the elephant's shoulder blades under my feet beneath the canopy of the singing jungle.

From the mournful wind instruments old as Siam itself to the little bending wrists of the Thai dancers.

From the serene face of the Buddha to the flower laden frangipani trees growing freely among the ruins left by the Burmese invasion.

From the upturned face of a Thai baby on my lap to the song of the giant night insects.

The peace of the temple, the peace of the mountains, the peace of the ocean.

I am lulled by it; I unfold in its presence and warm my aching, broken wings within its glow.

THAT DAY IN THE PARK

The sun filtered its rays through canopy of leaves in the park. Ribbons of light painted a kaleidoscope of patterns on the sandy path beneath her feet. Groups of small birds no longer breaking the silence of the green asylum in loud disagreements, chirped quietly about the difficulties of approaching winter.

October sprawled in the field lazily surveying his earthly domain and, feeling momentarily benign, allowed the sun to send down one of the last Indian summer days within the golden alleyways of the park. Leaves, dressed in yellow, red and orange robes of autumn twirled silently and settled on the path before her as she walked. They rustled and hummed in the warm fall air pushed aside by her tall leather boots.

She stopped briefly and inhaled the waning scents of summer, delighting in the surprising smell of burning leaves suffusing the air, and bringing her back to childhood days spent in the country.

She saw him before he saw her and, even though they had made this date to meet, she felt startled as she watched him draw near. It had been one year since they last saw each other and, although the pain of their parting had started to dissipate, here in this park, in the waning light it all came back to her. She felt like she would drown in the emotion and stopped to take control, to breathe and to fight the tightening of her throat.

He had not changed. Tall and trim, walking with that determined stride she knew so well, he sported a leather jacket and faded denim jeans. She could not see his eyes behind the aviator sunglasses and that unnerved her for a moment, for she remembered moments in the past when she thought she would drown pulled into the dark pools of those eyes.

Within a second he was near and without hesitation took her in his arms. Her head felt dizzy and she almost lost her balance, but he held her fast murmuring her name as he buried his face in her hair. She breathed him in; she breathed in that familiar scent of his skin, his hair, his cologne, and memories flooded her mind.

They made love everywhere in those long abandoned days: on the balcony of the resort, on the pier at sunset, in the ocean and on the beach at night. They made love on the stairs; to impatient to reach the bed they scattered clothes on each step. Their passion for each other was all encompassing and it never changed in the five years they spent together.

He always said that life was all about timing, but timing was not a friend of theirs and slowly the frustration set in ripping their lives apart. All that was left was the memory of something so special and so sacred that it had branded its visage on their very souls.

They stood there wrapped up in each other, unaware of sights and sounds around them. Was it for a moment? Was it for an hour? She could not tell. Slowly they moved apart, and she began to shiver. He took off his leather jacket and placed it around her shoulders. Now she was surrounded by his warmth, and scent, and love. Sitting down on a nearby bench they told each other of the changes in their lives. Like two old friends, the two lovers basked in each other's presence losing track of time, unaware of the waning autumn light.

The sun began to set and once again it was time to part. She stood up and took off his jacket handing it to him reluctantly. Somehow, that gesture held a note of finality; her heart started to beat faster and she felt her mouth go dry. He held her one more time and whispered that he loved her.

And then he walked away.

Tears sprung to her eyes, and for a moment his was just a blurry figure growing smaller in the distance. She stood there watching, but he did not turn around.

She had no way of knowing at that moment that they would never meet again.

THE CRAZIES - AUGUST 1977

It is only with the passage of time that we realize that those days which seemed so unending, so confining, were days filled with the tapestry of experiences which we would inevitably long for at a much later date.

I've had the crazies for three days now – getting worse and worse.

The morning starts off with the usual feeding and dressing routine.

When the children are done, I long for five minutes of alone time.

As I sit on the bed putting on my socks, my son copies my every move. Attached by that invisible umbilical cord, he follows me up and down the stairs until I beg him to let me have my tea.

He doesn't buy that.

Sitting on the same chair, his toast buttered next to mine, his teacup touching mine, we learn the deep meaning of the words "to share".

The laundry room, tucked deep in the guts of the house, seems like a great place to hide. I run downstairs and stuff the laundry into the machine.

It takes it all in like a glutton.

Tiny steps on the stairs-tiny hands on my thigh. He wants to watch the clothes mysteriously swishing around.

Another discovery.

Nina, my baby girl is hollering upstairs for the warmth of my body-for the cradle of my arms...

There is nowhere in the house I can go.

I feel the need to create-to let the pressure out from behind my heart. The answer seems to be hidden in music. Schubert has a way with music. I sit at my piano and begin the Serenade.

What's this?! A tiny tinkling at first-a loud toy piano-getting louder by the minute. A little voice singing: "Twinkle, Twinkle Little Star."

The tears in my throat change to laughter; it's all so absurd.

My fingers start to trip over one another. Schubert has lost his dignity. I stop.

Tiny hands clap with approval.
I start to laugh, the music gone from my soul.
I pick up my son and hold him to my heart.

THE DARKNESS

She slid the card into the keycard lock and entered as the door closed quietly behind her. Kicking off her high heels she sank her aching feet in the plush carpet of the stateroom and wiggled her toes.

The Penthouse Suite was dimly lit casting shadows on the sumptuous furniture; the butler must have turned on the soft lights for the evening. She noticed the silver ice bucket on the grand piano with a bottle of Bollinger Blanc de Noirs champagne which she ordered earlier.

It was their fifth wedding anniversary, and this was to be a celebratory nightcap as they enjoyed the star-studded Mediterranean night on the sprawling veranda of the Penthouse Suite. And it was the last-ditch effort to save their failing marriage. She planned the trip carefully choosing a well-appointed luxury liner and an interesting European itinerary.

They met in the fall of 2007. She was immediately attracted to him. Tall, slim with jet black hair and blue eyes he worked the bar like a magician pouring drinks from great heights, flipping tumblers and charming the female guests with his wit.

Women flocked to him and vied for attention, ordering more drinks than they should for the opportunity to linger at the bar and flirt with this charismatic bartender.

His name was Dominic. He came from Sicily with his parents and a younger sister at the age of five. The family was poor and struggling to make ends meet for most of his young life. A higher education was never in the cards for Dominic and, after high school, he began to search for work.

He had a variety of jobs from an attendant at the car wash to pizza delivery man and for a while he worked in his uncle's meat deli as a butcher. One day a friend who worked at the posh Boulevard Club told him about a bartender course and Dominic's future was set.

On the evening they met she had just concluded an unsuccessful relationship with a son of her father's business acquaintance and, although the match pleased her parents, the two were so diametrically opposed that no amount of effort could make one understand the other.

They tried to retain their relationship for a year, but their personalities could not mesh; Robert was brilliant in business but completely unaware of what makes a woman tick. In bed he was quick and completely self-absorbed.

On a cool November evening she asked him to meet her at the Boulevard Club and sustained with a vodka martini broke the news to him as gently as she could. He took it well; perhaps he knew that this relationship had absolutely no future left.

Her father on the other hand took the news very badly.

"What were you thinking?" he sputtered when she gave him the news. "You could have had a great future with Robert".

There was no point getting into the discussion of "whys" and "wherefores". This was her decision, and it was made.

That very evening, while sitting at the bar, she watched the charismatic bartender (a fine specimen of male pulchritude and sex appeal) and she decided to comfort herself with a one-night stand.

The sex was fantastic - better than she ever experienced in her life, and she was hooked.

They met often and ended up in bed each and every time until one day out of the blue he sprung "that" question on her.

Completely side-swiped, she stammered and blushed trying to weigh his proposal of marriage.

Her father would be furious. This was not an appropriate social pairing. She came from a family well known for their social connections and multi-million-dollar bank accounts.

The first two years of their marriage were good. They fought loudly and often both having strong personalities, but each fight was resolved in the bedroom with great verve and panache. Forgiveness was always just a roll in the hay away.

Nevertheless, things were beginning to unravel.

Dominic was slowly sucked into the dark and murky vortex of gambling and spent not only hours, but days, playing poker. He had no qualms decreasing the contents of their joint bank account regardless of how many times she begged him to stop.

The cruise was to be their chance at another life; a chance to be together, to experience the good life that they had the fortune of enjoying. Yet here she was, alone in the spacious stateroom, while he ordered drink after drink in the casino as he played endless hands of poker.

Tonight brought on the worst fight that they ever had and for the first time she told him that she had enough; enough of his drinking, his gambling, and his flirting with all the young and pretty women who inevitably were drawn to his dark charms.

Tonight she told him that she wanted a divorce.

And now she stood leaning on the grand piano and wondering what the rest of her life would look like.

A noise from outside caught her attention. She walked through the large sliding doors of the veranda and listened. Somewhere below two people were arguing loudly and for a moment she thought that she heard the voice of her husband.

"It can't be," she thought. "Surely it can't be."

Curious, she leaned over the railing and looked down. She could almost see the veranda below. Just five more inches and she would see who was in this melee. She put her foot on the lowest rung of the balcony and clutching the railing lifted herself up.

Suddenly she felt something, or someone hit her in the back between the shoulder blades. The hit was so strong that before she could understand what was happening her hands slid off the railing and she felt herself tumbling and plummeting towards the inky darkness of the sea.

She slammed into the water with a force that took her breath away. Disoriented, she continued to sink and plunge deeper into the sea. The salty brine stung her eyes so she shut them tightly praying for air. Her lungs felt like they would explode. Her mind was whirling; unable to put any thought together while the body struggled for survival.

After what seemed like an eternity she broke through the surface. Sputtering and coughing, her lungs desperately tried to expel the liquid intruder, this dark precursor to death.

She felt something brush by her leg and she panicked, sinking again into the darkness. The salt water stung as she inhaled it. At last, regaining the ability to stay on the surface she realized that she must call for help.

Screaming as loud as her voice would allow she wailed her S.O.S., intermittently floating and sinking beneath the murky brine. The night, illuminated by the moon with its silvery beams shining on the soft swells of the ocean, was an eerily beautiful witness to the horror-story at hand.

The ship continued on its course creating a shimmering wake, its twinkling lights growing smaller and dimmer in the night.

She bobbed up and down like cork in the increasing swells of the immense ocean noting the dark clouds gathering above her until they covered the bright face of the moon.

The ship was now just a dot on the horizon.

THE DOG

There once lived a dog--a fine, strong and proud dog whose name was "Love".

The dog lived in a small house with a little girl where life flowed uninterrupted and uneventful.

One day a Man came to the house and saw the dog, and loved the dog, and fed the dog scraps from the table. At first, the dog backed off and growled baring his teeth but the Man, undaunted, kept talking to the dog in soothing tones and the dog grew to trust the Man and in time, to love him.

Days turned into nights, nights into dawns and so it went. The dog would wait at the window for the Man to greet him with the "dance of the tail" and lick the Man's hands. And they would go outside where the Man would throw the red ball while the dog would catch it in his teeth and run back to the Man until the Man laughed and said: "no more".

Later the dog would lie beside the Man while the Man scratched the dog's ears and the very good spot on the dog's back just above the tail. And the dog would close his eyes and lay his head on the Man's knees for more scratches and more pats.

Then, after the Man fed the dog again, the dog would sleep at the Man's feet and dream of chasing rabbits in flower filled meadows where larks sang their summer songs. And his legs would twitch, and he would smile his dog smile. And when the dream was over he'd awake to see the Man dozing in the armchair. Then the dog would close his eyes again, happy and calm and content.

Days turned into months, then into years. The Man's absences grew longer. The dog would pace in front of the window and growl at the shadows made on the wall by passing headlights.

But the Man did not come back.

The dog would go outside and sniff into the wind, but the Man's scent did not come.

The neighbours would see the dog sitting in the window at sunset, the red ball at his feet. Other men came to the house and gave the dog food which he took because he was very hungry. But his eyes grew dull and his fur matted, and he would not lie at these men's feet or play with them with his red ball.

A decade passed. The dog never forgot the Man.

And one day the dog walked for a very long time following instinct and longing, and came upon a house, and smelled the very good scent of the Man.

So he yelped in despair-delight, and the Man came outside.

The reunion was grand. The dog bounded around the Man like a rabbit and they rolled in the grass together and hugged and licked, and the light came back into the dog's eyes. And when the day was done the Man started to go into the house and the dog followed. But the Man held up his hand and said: "Go home, I will come some day and bring you scraps".

The dog sat down surprised and cocked his head trying to understand.

The Man went towards the house and the dog followed. But the Man said: "I already have a dog in the house, and you have to go because blood is thicker than water. I will come and feed you scraps someday."

The Man went inside. And the dog understood and hung his head. He stood looking at the house for a long time, but the Man did not come out again.

It started to snow, and the streetlights came on, and the lights came on inside the house. The neighbours across the street could see the gray outline of a dog sitting on the lawn. The night passed. A salt truck passed by spraying salt everywhere. Only then did the dog get up as he slowly began to walk away.

He turned and looked at the house one more time, but it was dark and still.

So the dog walked without destination, his paws bleeding and cracked from the salt and snow, his whiskers covered in ice. His tail hung sadly between his legs.

Suddenly he heard a girl's voice calling his name. She hugged and scolded him at the same time for running away, and the dog knew that she loved him and he couldn't let her down.

He went home with the girl and lived a quiet life for another year or so. But when he dreamt, his dreams were of the Man, his laughter, the comfort of his hands, the peace of their afternoon slumbers and joy of their rollicking play.

THE HOMECOMING

Eight months and three weeks ago, my youngest brother Andy, who is an officer in the Royal Regiment of Canada, left for a mission in Afghanistan.

The purpose of this mission was to continue training the Afghan National Army in drill, range practice, patrolling techniques, checkpoint procedures and convoy exercises as well as protocols and procedures in order to take control of the country's security upon the withdrawal of the NATO troops in 2014.

He was stationed in Camp Alamo.

Camp Alamo was located on the outskirts of Kabul, directly across the street from the French Warehouse. It was situated in the boundary of Kabul Military Training Center. Hence the name "The Alamo". It was surrounded by ten thousand Afghans.

He lived in a 6' x12' "container on the military base and, as an officer, he had the luxury of having the container to himself.

On November 14th, 2012, he and his group came home.

The trip from Afghanistan took several days as it included a three day stay and "decompression" in Cyprus.

Alter 23 hours in transit, he finally arrived at the Trenton base where his wife, our mother, myself and my husband Steve awaited his arrival with our hearts in our hands. We were soon joined by his friend Greg, a sergeant in the Peel police, who would take us on an incredible journey of welcome and surprise.

The soldiers trickled out of the "arrivals" door one by one.

This was the first mission where not one single life was lost. That in itself was a cause for celebration.

Finally, Andy arrived. Many hugs and much applause later we piled into our cars and were told to follow the police sergeant out of Trenton.

My brother and his wife were in the first car and my husband and I immediately behind them.

The convoy was small. Our flashing four way lights allowed us to fly down the highway behind the police cruiser as people moved to give us the right of way.

As we turned off Brock Road onto highway 407, we noticed six police cruisers sitting on the side of the road. The moment we turned, their flashing lights came on and they placed themselves around us. But that was just the beginning.

Driving on, we noticed lots of flashing lights on the overpasses. There stood Fire Trucks and the fire fighters who were lined up on the bridge saluted as we drove by. Overpass after overpass, the flashing lights and the saluting men and women made us choke up with emotion. Some bridges held ambulances and police cruisers.

We stopped counting the overpasses after 11.

As I looked out my widow, I noticed a very bright light in the sky. At first, I thought it to be the moon but it was too bright, and it was moving. Then I thought it to be a plane, but it was too bright to be a plane as well.

A helicopter.

Could it be? No that's impossible!

But it was.

Its beam flowed towards the earth and our small convoy. Andy's car was in the beam of the helicopter for the duration of the trip.

Feeling like we had entered another strange dimension or at least a set of a Steven Spielberg movie, we came off the highway and headed towards Andy and Donna's Newmarket home.

Again, on the overpass that we entered stood two fire trucks and several police cruisers all awash in their coloured flashing lights.

Saluting, the fire fighters and police officers stood at attention.

Every intersection that we entered was blocked off by police so we did not have to stop at red lights. Also, each police officer stood saluting as we passed.

This was only a precursor to what we saw when we entered the street and pulled up to my brother's house. Police cruisers, ambulances and fire trucks lined the streets, and their flashing lights lit up the night sky in overwhelming colours.

The neighbours were out waiting in the frigid night. Children were holding up welcoming placards. Flowers were handed to Andy and Donna.

One little girl held up a sign with "Welcome Home, Andy". The sign was surrounded with little flashing white lights.

The lawn was lined with small Canadian flags, and people waved the flags they held in their hands. On the garage door, there was a huge sign with "Welcome Home" on it, and both the garage and front doors had posters with children's' pictures of army life. It was the cutest thing!

Much hugging, hand shaking, and photos taken with our hero took place when suddenly the crowd broke out in the National Anthem.

I don't know how one could remain untouched.

He's home now. Safe and sound. Away from the dust, dirt, bad food, but most of all, away from the constant danger of attack and the sheer uncertainty of discerning which one of the Afghan people is your friend, and which one your enemy just waiting to kill as many of you as he possibly can.

And to the beautiful people of Canada, all the men and women who showed such love and respect, who stood in the cold saluting one single soldier to thank him for his work, to all those people we send our thanks from the bottom of our hearts.

God Bess Canada.

THE KNEE

Knee(ne)-the site of articulation between the thigh(femur)and leg, also called GENU

I know that I shall never see
A joint as lovely as a knee.
Whether they're mine, or yours or theirs
Knees usually tend to come in pairs.
A famous king once said with glee:
"I'll give my kingdom for a knee"
(It wasn't a knee, you know of course,
Desired object was a horse...)
One thing at last I might contend
Without the knees, your legs don't bend.

Knees come in very handy from the day we are born. Babies are happy to kick their legs for hours and play with their feet. Without knees their little heels would develop little blisters and become calloused from hitting the mattress. And imagine wanting to play with your toes to pass the time and not being able to reach them?

As infants we learn to walk by first crawling on our hands and knees. In the absence of knees we would crawl depending solely on our elbows thus giving us a jump on training for guerrilla tactics, which would probably cause a great overflow in the world's armies and lead to war as a way of life.

Knees are a common site of scrapes, cuts and bruises, as they break our fall out of trees, off bicycles, over undone shoelaces, and later in life, off balconies of assorted fair and not so fair ladies. Without knees to break the fall we would knock out a lot of teeth, giving dentists more reason to stand in line on their way to their Swiss bank accounts.

Knees are commonly used for crossing.

Knee crossing (unlike deer crossing, which still needs working on)is a fine art developed to perfection over the years by those who sport the skirt, the hemline of which, by the way, is always judged by how much above or below the knee it falls.

Knee crossing (like deer crossing in this case) has often caused road accidents and has contributed to drinking problems. It has also been utilized effectively in pantyhose commercials and car ads.

Knees, next to the elbows, are strong contenders for the all-encompassing rug burn. The elbow-knee combo rug burn can be displayed proudly in locker rooms as a sign of endurance and immunity to pain. Displayed only on the knees it can be a sign of an active imagination. Displayed only on the elbows it is a sign that the owner of these elbows has most likely worked in a circus in the past.

The knees are a must for devotees, and are exercised at will and in unison by priests who know how to make 650 people fall upon them by merely ringing a bell.

In order to show humility, beg for forgiveness or to become a knight, one must have at least one well-functioning knee.

The knee is also known well throughout centuries as an object with which to fall upon a cushion and humbly ask for the adored-one's hand in marriage.

The knee contains a knee-cap which, unlike other caps, cannot be unscrewed or popped open with a bottle opener by anyone other than Uncle Vito, who has made this his forte.

The back of the knee is good for kissing and applying perfume and vice versa.

Lastly, imagine a world of people without knees.

Without knees, there would be no laps to sit on, climbing stairs would become another insurmountable problem.

In subways legs would stick straight out into the isles making manoeuvering down them impossible.

Without knees a squat would become obsolete so that we would have to lie down to pet small children and kiss dogs. Skipping would become bouncing, and getting into a bubble bath would become life-threatening.

And how would we know how far to pull up the knee socks without cutting off the circulation to the toes?

In summary, I would like to say that knees, whether bony or dimpled, whether quiet or creaky make our lives more comfortable, less complicated, and decidedly more exciting.

THE LATE SHIFT

I was approaching fourteenth hour of my double shift at the hospital.

As the only radiological technologist on the evening shift I had surely earned my keep that evening; the requisitions kept coming off the printer one after another.

"Finally, a moment of respite" I thought. "Hurray!"

I sat down at the front desk revelling in the momentary quiet when the printer sprung to life again.

"Oh, for Pete's sake! Nooooo!" I muttered to myself. It was a request for a STAT portable Chest X-Ray in "Resus".

"Resus" was short for Resuscitation Room. It was a room where critical cases where placed as it had complete monitoring equipment and a "Crash Cart". It was located in the very heart of Emergency.

"Great" I thought. "A critical case to end my shift."

Begrudgingly I rolled out the portable X-Ray machine and rumbled down the corridor to the Emergency area. The Emergency corridor was packed with patients and their families and the sight of blood, vomit, tears, and downright terror on the faces of a few people was a sign that all was normal in the world I had willingly entered many years ago.

As I turned my machine towards Resus I saw an old man sitting outside of its doors. He held a woman's coat on his lap and absentmindedly squeezed it with gnarled hands as if he was kneading dough. For a moment, our eyes met, and in his faded blue eyes I saw a pleading, a silent prayer and fear.

I quickly looked away and got on with business at hand.

Inside Resus an elderly woman lay on a stretcher. Her wavy gray hair formed a halo around her head. Her flannel nightgown was the colour of faded tea roses and on her left hand an old wedding ring cut into the ring finger disfigured by arthritis. She was hooked up to all the monitors which displayed the usual parameters of the patient's vital signs including heart rate, blood pressure, pulse oximetry and respiratory rate.

I walked up and bent over her. "Mrs. McKinnon I'm going to take your Chest X-Ray". I said quietly.

"O.K. My dear" she replied softly.

There was something immensely calm about her; something that required gentleness and a soft approach. I rolled the hulking machine closer to the stretcher and swung the arm of the X-ray tube over the woman.

Suddenly, the vital sign monitor sounded its certain alarm and glancing at it, I saw that the line of the heart rate became erratic. In a moment, a shrill sound from the monitor announced a flat line. Her heart had stopped.

I had to move quickly to get my heavy machine away from the bed as within seconds the room teemed with nurses, and doctors. The "Crash Cart" was rolled next to the patient as the Respiratory therapist began the intubation and started the manual ventilation process.

The emergency physician placed the defibrillator on the woman's now exposed chest and, after the words: "clear", administered the shock.

Her frail body arched backwards and sunk back into the bed.

The line on the heart monitor remained solid.

"Clear!" the doctor yelled and once again the shock sent the old woman forward and back again. The frustration in the room was growing-the urgency was increasing its pitch.

I had been a witness to this desperate fight to save another life many, many times.

For fifteen minutes the team tried in vain to bring back the escaping life, but that life had another path to embark on now.

The finality was met with silence and a quiet pronunciation: "Time of death: 2237 hours." I looked at the woman's face. It held neither fear nor regret. It was suffused with some sort of internal light. Her features softened and a slight smile seemed to alight on her lips.

"That's it then" I thought and reversed my machine out of the room. And then I saw the man.

He was not yet aware of what had transpired behind the closed doors of the room behind him. But I already knew the awful truth.

Once again our eyes met. His were red rimmed and moist with tears as if that truth had somehow seeped into his consciousness.

I looked away quickly.

I knew what would happen next. He would be called into the room with its curtain drawn around the stretcher where his wife lay. He would walk in holding her coat and be given the news. Then everyone would disappear while he was given the time to......

And then, he would go home.

He would enter the house so familiar to him for many years. The little black cat would greet him with his meowing. The table would be set just like they left it with two unfinished cups of tea and ginger snaps half eaten on the plate. He would look at the old armchair with her shawl that fell onto its seat and he would see the knitting on the floor- one tiny bootie finished: a gift for the new great grandchild.

He would see the pictures on the mantle; pictures of a family that grew from year to year, and his eyes would rest on that one picture of a young soldier with a pretty bride looking up at him with laughing eyes.

For many weeks the little black cat would lie on the fallen shawl draped on the chair waiting for the old woman to come home.

And life, as the old man knew it would never be the same.

I swung my X-Ray machine around the corner and parked it by the wall.

"Well, another day in paradise. The shift is almost over" my professional side grumbled.

And my human side covered its face and wept.

THE PARTHENON

I would like to walk up the endless steps of the Parthenon at four o'clock in the morning just to sit beneath its columns and listen to the silence of a thousand stories told by a thousand ghosts.

The greyness of dawn would lightly yield to coffee cup morning, stretching and yawning in the streets below still as a street mimes posing in the ruins.

The city would rise with traffic noises playing in my head; bicycle bells and car horns laughing.

Store keepers would unroll their awnings, marketplace-round- faces setting the fruit outside. Children, with morning traces of a milk moustache on their face, books peeking out of their knapsacks, knee socks neat and tidy, would tug at the temptation to spend the morning with the ducks in a nearby park.

Women, leaning on elbows in window frames and looking like they've been up for hours, would exchange cheerful hellos across the ivy taking the time to pass along a bit of gossip before the ironing wakes up with its demands.

The Parthenon bleached in the sunlight and still with a million deaths, shrill silence enveloping its columns lies waiting for the onslaught.

I sit enveloped in its womb of steps, curled into an embryonic form, feeling the dawn creep off my forehead like fever and spot the first two busses.

The tourists trickling in like insects huff and puff on their way up the white steps of the gods, searching around the corners for inspiration while fighting off local photographers and occasionally stopping to sip on a Coke.

The last lizard scampers across grumpily mumbling "I'm late..." provoking a shriek in its path.

The sun-baked temple, its columns sighing, watches in silence as it prepares once again to pose against the mass of rushing human flesh.

I rise out of my silence frowning at interruptions and gulping for air, lost in the ocean of blank stares, run down into the bosom of the city to greet the morning with some strong Greek coffee.

Looking up I see the Parthenon resembling old farmer Jones' bee-hive, with arms and legs and cameras and sunglasses all abuzz.

At the bottom, the line-up is buying tickets to the past.

THE RED STRING BIKINI

She couldn't put it off any longer; the long-awaited vacation was quickly approaching and packing of necessary clothes was a chore that she did not necessarily relish. And the least relished piece of clothing of all time was the bathing suit.

She knew that there was a modest black bathing suit which held in all the offending bulges while supporting the still pleasant ones and that was the one for which she rummaged around in the drawer. But what she pulled out was a tiny two-piece string bikini which lay there for many years, forgotten and forlorn. It was made up of four little (and I mean little!) red triangles held together with turquoise string.

And in that instant she was back on the powdery beach of Negril.

The beach was still fresh and unspoiled and the Negril Beach Club hotel on its periphery boasted two stories containing simple rooms, balconies with their overflowing banana trees which were host to spiders of considerable weight and girth, no electricity on Tuesdays (which heralded a party for the cockroaches in all places not illuminated), and a restaurant that served the best lobster dinners ever created by a human hand. On the beach the few tourists who stumbled upon this piece of paradise lay on bamboo chaises reading, sleeping, smoking dope, strolling along the beach, or lazily bathing in the blue-green sea.

Her body was lean and bronzed by the two weeks in the Jamaican sun and the little red bikini covered just enough to make it all interesting.

An old Jamaican man was walking slowly down the beach holding an aluminum bucket with freshly caught, barbequed lobster tails. This was a daily occurrence, and the tourists having once tasted the sweet meat provided the old man with brisk business. She got up from the lounge chair and headed towards the old man to buy her lunch.

As she passed the volleyball net a tall young black man accidentally backed into her.

Keeping her balance she scowled at him; however, at the same time she couldn't help noticing that he had the most perfectly sculpted, muscular body which glistened with sweat and oil.

As he caught sight of her, one word escaped from his lips: "Wow!"

Yeah. She was a "Wow" in that tiny bikini with her fit, bronzed body and long hair framing her young face.

She smiled a satisfied smile and turned away to find the man with the lobster lunch.

••••••••••

She didn't hear her husband come into the room as she stood holding that red bikini, lost in thought.

"Holy Cow!" her husband exclaimed. "Where did you get that? Whose is it?" He asked with a laughing voice. "Surely it can't be yours."

"No. no." She said. "I would look ridiculous in something like that. For heaven's sake, I'm a grandmother!"

THE SHOELACE

The June sun baked the city streets with unrelenting heat but, as they passed through the heavy iron gates of the park, a woman and a little girl breathed a sigh of relief.

The tall trees offered a much-needed escape from the sun's rays and the traffic noises were replaced with the constant chatter of birds, laughter of children and a distant sound of a waterfall.

The woman was tall and slim with chestnut hair and the greenest eyes you have ever seen. She wore a white dress with black polka dots, and her waist was cinched with a red belt. By anyone's standards she was a stunning beauty.

The girl of about three or four was dressed also in a white dress with a white and red pinafore. One hand clutched her mother's hand; in the other she held a much loved toy bunny.

They headed towards the pond where ducks vied for position with the majestic trumpeter swans as children threw bits of bread into the water.

The child let go of her mother's hand and headed towards the pond.

"Lalunia, wait a moment!" the mother called. "Your shoelace is undone". She walked up to the girl, bent down and tied up the rebel shoelace. As she got up, she smiled and softly said; "You are my sunshine, baby of mine" as she kissed the child's cheek.

•••••••••

The June sun baked the city streets with unrelenting heat but in the park the canopy of leaves offered much needed relief. The birds quarreled in treetops, children ran and played as parents looked on, and squirrels teased the passing dogs into a quick yet futile chase.

Two women strolled down the park lane, their arms entwined.

The older of the two appeared to be well into her eighties with hair as white as summer clouds and her back slightly bent with ravages of age. She walked slowly and on her face from time to time appeared a wince of pain. Years of living had left their mark, yet she seemed to be content and free of malice.

Suddenly, the young woman stopped and bent down on one knee "Your shoelace is undone" she said as she bent down to tie the rebel lace.

The old woman smiled. "Thank You Lalunia." She said quietly.

"You are my sunshine mama" I said as I kissed her cheek.

THE TWO WOMEN

I was the only baby on the ward born with a shock of thick black hair. By the time I was one month old, my mother would tie a big bow on top of my head just to keep the hair from getting matted. By the time I reached the age of seven, my hair reached to the middle of my calves.

I could never wear my hair down, as the slightest movement or a gust of wind would result in nasty tangles; therefore, my hair was always braided. I slept in braids, and every morning ritual included the combing and braiding of my thick tresses. It was my grandmother who was the caretaker of my hair. She was gentle and patient, beginning the combing process at the bottom and slowly working her way higher and higher with the comb, until my entire head was detangled. She would then braid my hair into two braids, each as thick as my arm, and intertwine a ribbon into the bottom of the braid then doubling it up and securing it with a bow behind my ears. The ritual would be followed by hot cream of wheat prepared by our nanny, and a walk to the bus stop where my grandmother would wait until the bus came, and wave to me as I began my journey to the music school which was situated clear across town.

My mother was diametrically opposed in character to my grand-mother.

As patient and calm as my grandmother was, so was my mother impatient, ebullient and energetic. I dreaded the times when, for what-ever reason she would take on the task of combing my hair, because she would grab the comb and begin not at the bottom but at the top of my head, demanding that the tangles yield under her ministrations, and causing me to yelp like a scalded puppy.

As a child of a former underground soldier, which my mother became during the war, I was taught never to whine, complain or otherwise show displeasure at the advent of pain. Even when my aunt Lila, who was a dentist, drilled my teeth with no anaesthetic, and occasionally hit a nerve, even then I could not cry. Crying was for sissies.

My mother did not have a mean bone in her body. She was just raised with incredible discipline doled out by her father. Her father, my grandfather, was an officer in the Polish army at the time when only the elite were allowed to reach that status. In his opinion, children were to be heard and not seen. They would behave in an exemplary manner at all times. They would strip to the waist in the morning and wash with cold water to harden the spirit. They would eat at the table with a knife and fork from the age of three, and never, but never would they be in the company of adults unless invited to play an instrument or sing a song.

My grandmother tried to soften this atmosphere by often breaking his rules, and allowing the children certain liberties when he wasn't looking.

My mother attempted to follow his teachings by imposing similar restrictions and rules upon me. At first, I complied. I curtsied when meeting an adult, I played the piano beautifully, I had good manners at meals and I used "please" and "thank-you" with great verve and panache. What happened when I reached teenage years, dear reader is a topic for another time.

But getting back to my grandmother, she was always my calm port in the storm. And if she was my calm port, my mother was a Star Clipper with sails unfurled. Always in a hurry, full of energy and laughter, she would hug and kiss me with such enthusiasm that my eyes would water. My grandmother, on the other hand, would stroke my hair gently and kiss me with calm tenderness.

The two women in my life, as different as they were, shared three incredible characteristics: courage, strength of survival and the knowledge that one must never give up.

My grandmother was a child of 16 when she married her first husband, a man 20 years her senior. She bore him three children: two girls and one boy. Her life was full of privilege and comfort. There were estates and servants to see to her every need. Years later, after her first husband's death, she married my grandfather and had two more children, a boy and the youngest child, a girl, who later became my mother.

The halcyon years of her youth would soon come crashing down, as war made its unwelcome presence. Her two older daughters, who were already married with children of their own, were sent to a concentration camp in Oświęcim, renamed Auschwitz by the Germans. (Many years later, as we made our life in Canada, we heard that her oldest boy, my uncle Władek, while travelling on business was one of the unfortunate passengers on a civilian plane that was shot down over the Sinai desert by the Israeli air force.)

After the horror and crushing grief of her daughters' deaths, my grandmother stepped up to the plate to lose herself in conspiracy, the headquarters of which were in the wartime apartment located ironically an few hundred feet from a German post. It's always safest where it is thought to be insanely unsafe, I learned later.

Because of this unstable and dangerous situation, my grandmother decided to send my mother to the care of a friend of hers who was a commander in the Polish underground. It was a hard decision for her, but a potential life saver for my mother. There, in the forest, life began for my 16 year old mother. Nothing could have prepared her for what was in store. No one could have warned her of the cold, the damp, the fear, the blood, the death, the ambushes, the night relocations, the lice, the hunger, the longing for even a tiny smattering of a normal life. She learned to walk while asleep, with her hand hooked into the belt of the soldier in front of her. She learned to take apart, clean and put together a rifle which she also learned to use.

She learned to dip a stick in the fire, and with its glowing tip to burn the lice off the backs of her compatriots. She learned that because you have become good friends with one boy, you must put those feelings aside when you find him shot with his eyes gouged out. She learned about the swift forest justice as a soldier that was found to be a spy for the Germans was brought back to camp and unceremoniously shot in the back of the head. She learned that just because you found a nice comfy ditch to sleep in didn't mean that you won't wake up covered in mud and water as the rains come in.

And so passed her teenage years. No prom dresses, no makeup lessons, no hand holding in a darkened movie theater, no sodas with girlfriends in a nearby café, no walks in a park on a sunny spring day. No Christmas around the family table, or birthday cakes. Not even the dreaded school exams.

Yet there were many more trials to follow.

As a soldier in what is now called "The Home Army", my mother with her colleagues continued to oppose the Russians as they came in to "save us" from the Germans. This branded her as an enemy of the state. (Incidentally, after the fall of Communism, the Polish Home Army is now touted as heroes, an honour which came much too late for a great number of the soldiers.) Shipped out to Siberia, she escaped from the convoy. Taken to the wall by Russians to be executed, she was spared at the last minute. Taken out of our home by the SB in the middle of the night in 1951 and thrown into horrendous surroundings of a prison for 6 months, she managed to pull of another miracle and be released. And somehow, within all that she endured, my mother adopted an attitude that was a combination of courage, intolerance for anything unjust, belief in a better tomorrow as well as disdain for any self-pity.

And somewhere between the role model provided to me by two of these women, I tried to find my balance in life.

It has not always been easy.

Wielka Street

Krysia or "Kitty" was the youngest of five children of Zofja, a wonderful and noble Catholic woman born into the privileged class of prewar Poland. There were servants and estates to be run and the gentle Zofja was beloved by her friends as well as the servants whom she treated as her own family. Never having to cook or clean she was one of the many women whom one would assume to be spoiled and unable to fend for herself.

In 1939 the life she knew came to an abrupt and horrible end when Poland was invaded by the Germans, and shortly afterwards by its "friends" the Russians.

Instead of shrinking away from the scene around her, she and her two eldest daughters, Irena and Janina entered into conspiracy, eventually setting up their house situated several miles from the city of Warsaw as a main hub for the falsifying of passports for those in need, and the storage and distribution of weapons.

Irena's husband was taken away and executed by the Germans soon after the onset of the war in what was known as the Außerordentliche Befriedungsaktion, or Extraordinary Operation of Pacification, a Nazi German campaign aimed to eliminate the intellectuals and the upper classes of the Polish people and of Polish nationhood.*

Janina's husband was away fighting in the forests and the villages against the oppressor.

---

*The mass murder of Polish leaders, politicians, artists, aristocrats, the intelligentsia, and people suspected of potential anti-Nazi activity was seen as a pre-emptive measure to keep the Polish resistance scattered and to prevent the Poles from revolting during the planned German invasion of France. The anti-Polish campaign was prepared by Hans Frank, the commander of the General Government, and was also discussed with Soviet officials during a series of secretive Gestapo-NKVD Conferences
Ref: Noakes and Pridham, Nazism: A History in Documents, p. 965.

The quiet town of Zielonka was a perfect camouflage for the work being done by Zofja, Irena, Janina and the many volunteers who worked around the clock to save lives and put a cog in the deadly machine of the Nazi occupation.

In a horrible turn of events while Kitty and her mom were in Warsaw, the Germans, tipped off about the activities in the town of Zielonka, arrested the two women and their three children and took them to Pawiak, a dreaded Warsaw prison. From there, the women were transported to Auschwitz where they eventually died. The children were spared by the quick thinking of Zofja's eldest son who paid an undisclosed amount of money to have them released from Pawiak prison before the transport to Auschwitz. The children were told to walk away from the prison gates and not look back. Someone would come and get them. Irena's two children, a boy of 15 and a girl of 13, bravely pushed forward, but little 6-year-old Adam, Janina's son, sobbed and called for his mom.

The news of her daughters' internment shook Zofja to the core. She and the youngest Kitty were not safe; they were a target now. They were marked for death.

Connections were made and Zofja, through a co-conspirator, managed to find a safe place for her and Kitty in an abandoned apartment building on Wielka Street in Warsaw. This building, occupied by Jewish Poles before the war, now sat abandoned, as the Jews of Warsaw were rounded up and herded into a walled off area--the Jewish Ghetto.

The apartment was completely empty except for two single beds, but it was the last place anyone would look for these two wanted women. It was safe by virtue of its location.

The large concrete balcony offered Kitty a clear view of the Jewish Ghetto, and she could see all the activity, all the suffering and all the horror as it unfolded. She could also see that every day in the wall of the Ghetto appeared an opening where the bricks were removed. People appeared with produce and goods of all sorts. Serious bartering was taking place, and the ghetto hummed with activity.

Inside the Ghetto, a young man of about twenty or so caught Kitty's eye. At the young age of 18, caught in this awful war, she was unable to forge normal friendships and relationships. And so, between the balcony and the wall, the two struck up a friendship.

He told her that he was a sentry. His job was to watch out for the Germans as the bartering and exchange of goods took place. So every day she would come out on the balcony and they would talk as he kept a watchful eye on the surroundings.

One cloudy morning as the hole in the Ghetto wall buzzed with activity and Kitty and the young man chatted, she turned her head to see from her vantage point high on the balcony, several German soldiers hunched down, their rifles drawn and ready approaching the Ghetto. Someone must have tipped them off.

Frightened that they might spot her, she slunk as far back on the balcony as she could, nevertheless gesticulating madly to her sentry friend below with a silent charade showing him drawn guns.

He understood immediately. Within seconds, the hole in the wall disappeared and so did all the people on either side of it.

The Germans arrived to find absolutely nothing going on. They left without an incident, their rifles slung on their backs.

The next day, the young sentry beckoned for Kitty to come down to the Ghetto wall. She declined, telling him that she was afraid.

He insisted. Drawing up her courage, she ran downstairs and sidled up to the hole in the brick wall of the Ghetto. And through it, he slid a small box and a note.

She ran upstairs breathless and hopeful that she was not seen. In the box were wonderful, fragrant, baked cookies and the note said: "With heartfelt thanks for saving the lives of Jewish workers of the Ghetto."

Shortly afterwards, the Ghetto Uprising drew out the fury of the Germans who emptied it of its many inhabitants.

The Warsaw Uprising followed. Kitty and he mother had to flee the apartment, leaving behind the few belongings that they managed to keep, including the little box in which Kitty kept the note from the Jewish people of the Ghetto.

It was lost, or stolen, or destroyed. She would never know.

Years later, she would say to me: "That note was the most wonderful gift I have ever received, because if you can save even one human life you have not lived in vain."

Kitty was my mother; Zofja, my wonderful grandmother. I owe them a debt of gratitude for instilling in me courage, perseverance, and respect for life.